TAKE THAT
OUR GREATEST HITS

TAKE THAT
OUR GREATEST HITS

**Virgin Publishing would like to extend a special thank
you to the following people for their help with the book**

Nigel Martin-Smith and Soozii Walker @ NMS
Chris Healey, Tour Manager
Simon Kenton @ Idols
Louise Hart, Nij Walker, Jane Chapman and
Jill Paterson @ RCA Records
Kate Hodges for editorial research
Di Skinner for the transcriptions

First published in Great Britain in 1996
by Virgin Books
an imprint of Virgin Publishing Limited
332 Ladbroke Grove
London W10 5AH

A catalogue record for this book is available from the British Library

ISBN 1 85227 635 5

Printed and bound by Bath Press

Designed by Slatter~Anderson
For Virgin Publishing: Philip Dodd, Carolyn Price

C O N T E N T S

Hiya!

Welcome to our new book, which is all about our Greatest Hits, every single one of them. We sat down and just allowed ourselves to go back in time... It was great to do that because we recalled many many good memories that we've shared together and with you.

We've been pretty honest too, about the songs and videos we do and don't like quite so much, as well as some of the outfits we've worn from time to time which weren't completely flattering!

But most importantly we've been able to remember just how much fun we've had being Take That, recording and singing and dancing to some brilliant songs. And to help remind us, we've included the best photos from our archives, and the lyrics to the songs that we wrote.

Above all this book is a chance to say a big thank you personally to you for joining in our great adventure and giving us so much support and encouragement over the years.

One thing's for Sure, although Everything Changes, we'll Never Forget our fans.

THANK YOU.

Loads of love,

MY TOP THREE

- I like Back For Good: I can never have enough of that track. I could listen to it over and over again.
- Why Can't I Wake Up With You: particularly the remix version.
- Never Forget: because it's just about us - and the remix sounds fantastic too.

OUR MOST ROMANTIC

A Million Love Songs: I wrote that when I was sixteen, so it's got quite an innocent lyric. We've performed it at nearly every concert we've done, and the audiences seem to love it too.

GARY GB

BEST VIDEO

For content, I like the Never Forget video. There's just so much in there, so many reminders of good times we were having. For sheer quality then it's got to be Back For Good.

HITS THAT MIGHT HAVE BEEN?

I think we've always made good choices and put out our best tracks. I have no regrets about any of the songs that have or haven't been released. I think we've done it all pretty well.

SECOND OPINIONS

A couple of weeks before Back For Good was coming out we met George Michael and he thought it was going to be Number 1 for six weeks - so he was only out by two weeks, and it was a nice comment. And Elton John thinks Love Ain't Here Anymore is the best of our songs.

MEMORIES

I still enjoy hearing a lot of the songs, especially after a long time because it brings back memories of when we were in the studio. I can always remember where we were and what sort of day it was. Some of the songs make me cringe a bit, though, because I think my voice is much better now than it was then.

MOTHER'S PRIDE

My Mum's favourite would be Pray - because it was our first Number 1.

ONSTAGE FAVES

I generally like the ballads to perform live because I don't have to move around the stage much. So I always like doing Babe because Mark's having to sing it and there's no dancing. I'm literally doing nothing... so that's probably my favourite!

MY TOP THREE

- **Babe: because it inspired me to play guitar.**
- **Back For Good: definitely one of the classics.**
- **Pray: superb song, brilliant routine, great video.**

ONSTAGE FAVES

I like the uptempo ones because I like to dance - you know, I like to shift a bit. And Babe and Back For Good where I can get on the old guitar.

HITS THAT MIGHT HAVE BEEN?

Give Good Feeling would make a great single and two songs called Still Can't Get Over You and Mr Blue. I doubt we'll ever release any of them but I love them all, as it happens.

MY FAVOURITE THINGS

JASON JO

BEST VIDEO

It Only Takes A Minute was the most enjoyable to make because the whole thing of making videos was relatively new to us and we were all excited by all the ideas.

MEMORIES

It's good to listen to the really early songs because they remind myself and the group that we've not always been that good. Some people would argue that we're still not that good, as it goes...

SECOND OPINIONS

Chris Lowe from the Pet Shop Boys said he liked the way we have different dance routines for different songs - and I told him I like the way he had different shades and hats in all their videos.

MOTHER'S PRIDE

I think my Mum is still waiting ever so patiently for me to sing one. And when and if that happens I reckon that might be her favourite, however unusual it sounds! Off the Greatest Hits album she'd say Back For Good.

OUR MOST ROMANTIC

Babe is beautiful: I love all that hero returns home stuff which is what the song is all about.

- **Once You've Tasted Love:
  I just loved the whole thing
  from listening to Gary's
  demo through to the
  end result.**
- **Why Can't I Wake Up With You:
  the remix by the Jervier brothers –
  again lots of memories, a great
  experience.**
- **Back For Good: a classic song that
  definitely crossed over to a wider
  audience, and brought us more
  worldwide success.**

BEST VIDEO

Why Can't I Wake Up With You holds so
many memories of going to Paris and staying
in that château. We enjoyed ourselves so much
all the time we were there that it was a little
bit sad to have to leave.

MOTHER'S PRIDE

Knowing my Mum her favourite would be a soppy
one: A Million Love Songs or the first version of
Why Can't I Wake Up With You.

OUR MOST ROMANTIC

**I think Babe really has to be the most
romantic song – if you listen to the
words they explain it all.**

ONSTAGE FAVES

The song I prefer to sing on stage is Why Can't
I Wake Up With You, where Gary and me take
turns on different verses. But the one that tops the
lot is Never Forget, not just because I sing it, but
because of the crowd reaction: the biggest buzz
I've ever had on stage.

HOWARD

 MY FAVOURITE THINGS

MEMORIES

**I was watching Top Of The Pops the other day and
they were running an old tape of us doing It Only
Takes A Minute. We all looked so different, but I got
right back into the song. It's really a pleasant surprise
to hear the old singles again.**

HITS THAT MIGHT HAVE BEEN?

As far as friends and family go, they're always complaining to me and saying 'Why don't
you release If This Is Love?' Although I wrote it, with me not having much confidence, I
simply tell them it's not good enough to be a single, though they all seem to think it is. A
lot of people have come up and said we should release Another Crack In My Heart,
which is a beautiful song. And a personal favourite of mine would be Nobody Else.

- **Back For Good: obviously one of the top three songs for me.**
- **Never Forget: a very emotional song and one that involves the audience a lot.**
- **Sure: great dance routine and another good one to perform live.**

BEST VIDEO

My favourite video is Never Forget because of all the scenes of me and the boys backstage - but I'm biased because I helped direct it. And Babe is well done because it takes you through a story, like a mini film.

HITS THAT MIGHT HAVE BEEN?

On the Nobody Else album there were lots of contenders for singles but with everything that happened, we just wanted to get back into the studio and start again... I like The Day After Tomorrow, although the lyrics are quite sad, and Give Good Feeling off our first album is a great uptempo song and great to perform live.

MY FAVOURITE THINGS

MARK

ONSTAGE FAVES

Sure and Never Forget and, of course, Babe, the song I first sung as a solo, although I usually get nervous doing that one.

MEMORIES

When I hear the earlier songs, I must admit some of them sound a little dated, but it is always a nice surprise to hear them on the radio. It brings back memories. Every song has a different memory.

SECOND OPINIONS

A lot of my friends like Back For Good because they think the video is pretty cool and the period of that song holds good memories. And A Million Love Songs because when they close their eyes and listen they can see us back at Flicks in Huddersfield - our first ever gig.

MOTHER'S PRIDE

My mum loves the ballads so her list would include A Million Love Songs, Babe and Back For Good. She doesn't like songs like Sure although after a while I think they grow on her, like fungi or something.

OUR MOST ROMANTIC

Why Can't I Wake Up With You, especially in the original Take That and Party version.

OUR FIRST EVER SINGLE. WE WERE ALL SO EXCITED WHEN IT WAS RELEASED. LOADS OF NEW EXPERIENCES: STUDIO SESSIONS, VIDEO SHOOTS AND RADIO PLAYS. WE HAD NO IDEA JUST HOW FAR WE'D GO FROM HERE.

Do What U Like

Music & lyrics **GARY BARLOW AND RAY HEDGES**   Lead vocal **GARY**   Release date **JULY 1991**   Highest UK position **82**

THE FIRST TIME WE HEARD THE SINGLE PLAYED WAS ON RADIO 1. SIMON BATES WAS PLAYING IT AND WE JUST CHEERED FOR THREE AND A HALF MINUTES.

Jason I was the only member of the group who thought it would be a massive hit. When we listened to the charts the lads lost heart when Number 10 had been announced and we'd still not entered the charts. I was so sure we'd go in at Number 1. It got down to Number 3 and then Number 2 and I thought 'Yeah, it's going in at Number 1'. As it happened it only went in at Number 82...

Gary I wrote it with a guy called Ray Hedges who's gone on to work with people like Boyzone. I prefer writing on my own though. A good fun record.

Howard This was probably one of the easiest songs to sing because all we had to do was say 'Do what you like' and 'Cherry pie' and all the different words. A good experience to be in the studio with a set of headphones on.

Mark When we were recording it, I kept getting the words mixed up - it was all very confusing.

I DIDN'T SLEEP THE NIGHT BEFORE BECAUSE I WAS SO ANXIOUS FOR THE SHOOT TO GO WELL. I FANCIED THE GIRL IN THE VIDEO - NICOLA. SHE WAS A BABE, BUT I THINK SHE FANCIED HOWARD. HE'S GOT A FLIPPING TOP BUM, YOU KNOW, AND I THINK SHE TOOK A LIKING TO THAT. **JO**

Howard It was a very tiring day: we did the routine hundreds of times, from 8 in the morning to about 12.30 at night. For months afterwards we still had jam and ice cream stuck in our ears which we couldn't get out even with the best cotton buds.

Mark I remember taking my clothes off in front of all these strange people and thinking 'What have I got myself into and what will my Mum and friends say?'

Gary Very exciting because we just wanted to see our names on the record. So good.

Howard I don't know why on earth they put my photograph at the top and bigger than everyone else. I don't know whether Gary was angry about it.

HOWARD WAS AT THE TOP AND I WAS AT THE BOTTOM AND I WANTED TO BE WHERE HE WAS... ONLY JOKING. **JO**

D O   W H A T   U   L I K E

D O   W H A T   U   L I K E

 Mark Do What U Like was the opening song on our first tour: I was crying the first time I heard the screams, whether with fear or joy I still ain't sure, so sure.

Howard An energetic routine: I think my favourite was the kick – you drop down on the floor, kick in the air, cross your legs and jump over onto your belly. One of the hardest for everyone to learn.

Gary I won't be sad to leave dance routines behind because, as you know, I'm not the best dancer in the world.

Jason I chose the clothes for this song and I still get regular abuse from the boys to this day.

Howard Well ladies and gentleman, boys and girls, dogs and cats, we are not to blame. If you want to complain about the leather and the codpieces please write to Jason.

Gary When we left those costumes in the cupboard, it was definitely our breakthrough time.

WE LOOKED LIKE A CROSS BETWEEN THE VILLAGE PEOPLE AND THE CHIPPENDALES. THE THINGS YOU DO FOR STARDOM... MO

Jason We performed Do What U Like on a roadshow one summer on an extremely hot day. Howard decided to do the performance barefoot, but the metal stage was so hot, his feet were burning – and it was the best I've seen him dance in all the years I've known him!

Mark Some of my memories of this song are jarred by the cans of beer that used to hit me on the head. Some of the audiences were kind enough to give us free beer, say no more.

Gary It was quite a tough time for us because were gigging all over the country. We were working really hard.

Sugar sweet, if only they all knew
Jam, can't spread no more you've took my bread
Energy, just work, no rest or play
Me, myself I'd rather be alone again

So you can do what you like (Do what you like)
No need to ask me (Do what you like)
Do what you like (Do what you like)
No need to tell me (Do what you like)

Cherry pie, you're not as cute as me
Ice, could never be as cold as you
Recipe, you stir me up inside
Me, myself I'd rather be alone again

Chorus (repeat twice)

BY OUR SECOND SINGLE, WE KNEW A LITTLE MORE
ABOUT RECORDING AND PERFORMING. WE WERE
GETTING MORE AIRPLAY, DOING TV SHOWS AND WE
HAD A RECORD DEAL WITH RCA. DEFINITELY A MOVE UP.

Promises

Music & lyrics **GARY BARLOW AND GRAHAM STACK**   Lead vocal **GARY**   Release date **NOVEMBER 1991**   Highest UK position **38**

Gary I wrote Promises with a fellow called Graham Stack. Then we re-recorded it with Pete Hammond, who made a pretty good job of it. We'd gone from having to record late at night to save money to now, all of a sudden, being able to take as long as we wanted.

Mark When we recorded the song with Graham Stack, he had this list of all the famous people he'd worked with. I was quite starstruck.

Howard We went down to London and I remember sitting with Peter Hammond, the producer, watching with interest, learning about songwriting.

Jason I was on the sunbed because I wanted to be browner than all the lads, and Gary especially. But then in walked Gary with the demo tape of this song, and I thought to myself 'Damn, it doesn't matter how brown I get, or how white he stays, because while he's writing songs like that he's always going to get the girls'.

Jason The five of us were all standing around one microphone in the studio, all shouting 'What you telling me that for' at the top of our voices. There was a right din but the producer loved it.

Howard It was all done on location in and around London. People were looking at us funny, wondering 'Who the hell are they?'

ALL THE WAY THROUGH THE SHOOT ROBBIE AND I WERE JUST MAKING EACH OTHER LAUGH, WE WERE CRYING WITH LAUGHTER. IF YOU LOOK CLOSELY YOU CAN SEE OUR EYES ARE RED.

Mark We had to arrive in this big daft limo at a club called Hollywoods in Romford where we'd performed a few times. Because we couldn't get it right we had to keep doing it and the gathering outside were booing us. So embarrassing.

Mark I seem to recall Howard thinking he looked like he'd been crying, and Gary was wearing my best shirt of the time. A black and white spotty number.

P R O M I S E S • P R O M I S E S • P R O M I S E S

Gary The dance routine was another Howard and Jason effort. When we used to live in the flat in Stockport, Jason was making the routine in the front bedroom... It had the hardest dance break we'd ever done. I was nearly blue when I came up to sing 'What you telling me that for' the last time.

Howard It was a tiring routine, because we had a break section in it – we had loads of dancing to do, and it was hard to catch your breath. Now we've learnt how to pace ourselves.

Jason With Howard's help I learned the back flip for this routine. I'd always been scared of doing it, but once I'd learnt it the lads had to restrain me because I was backflipping everywhere and wanted to put it in all the songs, even the ballads.

Howard It was a mistake to wear massive boots for such a fast-moving dance routine – they slowed everything down.

THE LEATHER HAD GONE

FOR A SORT OF RUBBER

BIKER JACKET. WELL, WE

DIDN'T WANT TO CHANGE

TOO QUICKLY, DID WE?

Howard On one tour, there was a move where I placed my foot in Mark's hand and he'd flick me over. One night in Berlin, my foot wasn't in his hands properly. I slipped, landed on my finger and dislocated it which was horrible. After that we didn't do the back somersaults.

Mark When Howard dislocated his finger, the hero returned about twenty minutes later with his finger in plaster to play the piano on A Million Love Songs. I still don't know how he did it.

Jason We performed Promises on the Wogan TV show. That made us really excited - and nervous - because we knew lots of people watched it. Uncle Terry Wogan was a top bloke. Made us feel relaxed: wibbly wobbly, wibbly wobbly.

Standing back I can't believe how you've led me on
And judging by the things you say
There's gotta be something wrong

What you telling me that for when you don't mean it
What you telling me that for I don't believe it
Your promises have never been anything you made them seem
So what you gonna promise me this time
You telling lies so plain to see
You're trying to make a fool of me
So what you gonna promise me this time
I wanna know

Seems like I've been playing your game
And how you think you've won
But when you count up what you've gained you're the lonely one

Chorus (repeat twice)

WE THOUGHT THIS WAS GOING TO BE OUR FIRST HUGE HIT, AND WERE REALLY GUTTED THAT IT DIDN'T DO ANYTHING.

Gary This was one of the most exciting stages of our recordings because they used so much of my original demo on this song. I thought 'God, I'm really getting to grips now with writing pop music'. It's basically about people who are about to fall in love and how they should take it easy.

Howard I was very disappointed that the single didn't do very well in the charts. I thought it would do better than all the others: a good dance song - it's still one of my favourites out of all the Take That songs. I was down in London with Gary when he played me the demo. I just kept rewinding it and listening and listening to it.

Mark We were driving through London going for an Indian and playing the track full blast. I thought the song was brilliant. Our vocals were improving and with Rob's rap on there I thought it was very up to date.

Jason The rest of the boys liked this song and I didn't think much of it to be honest. I thought it was a bit too techno.

Once you've

Music & lyrics **GARY BARLOW**   Lead vocal **GARY**   Release date **JANUARY 1992**   Highest UK position **47**

tasted love

WE WERE BECOMING THE MOST FAMOUS GROUP IN BRITAIN FOR NOT HAVING A HIT.

Howard I thoroughly enjoyed the recording of Once You've Tasted Love because it was a very musical song. I've always been good at putting harmonies on songs and I picked out a lot for this song, which made me very happy.

Gary We spent about two weeks recording which is actually quite a long time to record a song. We had it mixed by the fella who mixed KLF. He made a brilliant job of it. It has something that I just don't get tired of listening to.

Jason One of the hardest video shoots we've ever done. We had to perform the routine about fifty times. I didn't like the outfits and we had too much make-up on.

Mark By the time the shoot was over we were all completely knackered.

Howard At the end of the video shoot we let in the fans who'd been waiting outside. Every time we do a video shoot, we always have followers outside but we like to take them out a cup of tea and a biscuit because we're kind like that. Not the chocolate Hobnobs, though: I like to save them for myself. Just Rich Tea.

O N C E   Y O U ' V E   T A S T E D   L O V E

Jason I wasn't keen on the song, I disliked the video and I really didn't like the single artwork either.

Gary At this point we were pretty confused about what we needed things to look like and so it was a bit of a mixed up record.

Howard All five of us look as though we've just woken up, we must have had a bad night or something, and we've got about three inches of make-up on our faces.

Mark We all look shattered.

Jason We did Once You've Tasted Love on our first ever ticket tour and the crowd loved it; they loved singing along with the tune.

Mark We had a new choreographer in to do this routine and at first I must admit we all struggled, including Howard and Jason. Eventually though it came together - a good routine with lots of clever moves. A lot of the venues only had one or two microphones, so there was a lot of mike swapping going on for different parts of the song - very confusing, it was.

Howard I came to the front on one part and went into box splits which showed off my flexibility - I used to enjoy doing that because all the way through most of the girls would be looking at everybody else, and I thought here was my chance to show how long my legs were.

Mark The outfits for performing Once You've Tasted Love live were pretty much the same as Promises. I remember these big baggy black trousers I used to wear that a shop called Zutti made for me. I'd worked there in my younger years; lovely people.

Gary I remember when Rob recorded his rap on the song. We had to slow it down because he sounded like Mickey Mouse...

Don't be sold a dream
Remember how the past has been
Don't be led to believe this one's
for you
Calculate your needs
I see there's room to plant your seeds
Don't decide till you see how the others have grown

Once you've tasted love
It is just the beginning of a new world
Once you've tasted love
There's no way you can give in, oh no
Once you've tasted love

Still too early to know
Give them time and they will grow
Don't believe that the first one's the one for you
Most will grow to be tall
Others will break and fall
Keep your eye on the strongest head of them all

Once you've tasted love
It is just the beginning of a new world
Once you've tasted love
It is just the beginning, your head is spinning
Once you've tasted love

Once you've tasted love
It is just the beginning of a new world
Once you've tasted love
There's no way you can give in, oh no

You can't control your mind
And your head is still spinning, oh yeah
Once you've tasted love
It is just the beginning

Once you've tasted love
You've tasted love, you know it's good
Come taste my love, you know
you should

Rap

Come into my world as the badness disappears,
Take my hand, don't be afraid, I will work on all
your fears
They say so much and they give you only a glove
When I see your eyes I realise you too are made to love.

You've tasted love you know it's good
Come taste my love, you know you should.

EVERYTHING CAME TOGETHER ON THIS SINGLE. OUR FIRST REAL SUCCESS AND OUR FIRST TOP TEN HIT. WE ALL WORKED REALLY HARD ON THE PROMOTION, PERHAPS BECAUSE WE HAD A FEELING THIS WOULD BE THE ONE.

IT ONLY TAKES A MINUTE

Music & lyrics **DENNIS LAMBERT AND BRIAN POTTER**   Lead vocal **GARY**   Release date **MAY 1992**   Highest UK position **7**

Howard The first time I heard the song was in the office. We all sat down and listened to the version Tavares had done. To be honest I didn't really like it at the time, and I was worried that we needed the right single after Once You've Tasted Love which had been a bit of a flop. But our spirits were high once we started recording the song.

Gary It was a cover version we were all keen on doing. Good song, good pop song.

Mark I thought it was a catchy pop song, and our last chance to have a hit record.

Jason It had a good vibe, and I get excited when the rest of the lads get excited.

Howard The older generation remembered it from the first time, and the younger ones liked it because it's catchy.

Howard The track wasn't a hard one to sing. I think Robbie had a go at the lead vocal, but Gary's turned out to be a better one. Nigel Wright, the producer, was very quick. It varies sometimes with producers, they work in different ways, but he was very speedy.

Mark We recorded with a guy called Nigel Wright at his home; it was a lovely place with a swimming pool, very enjoyable.

Gary This was the time we went back out to really sell our name, Take That. Before Once You've Tasted Love we cut down on the gigs a bit, and so we just went back out to promote It Only Takes A Minute, doing signing sessions up and down the country. We did so much promotion for this record, we couldn't do one more single thing.

I THOUGHT ALL THE

DANCING LOOKED

EXCELLENT ON THE VIDEO,

AND WE ALL LOOKED GREAT. **GB**

H O W A R D

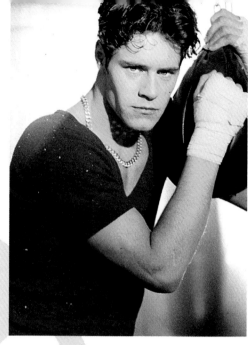

It was our first black and white video which I'd always wanted to do because you see so many other videos in black and white and you think 'Hey, that looks good'. The girl in the video was the sister of a guy called Patrick who used to be in Worlds Apart. Patrick was doing a bit of boxing training at the time although he wasn't in a group; I think he must have been inspired, gone away and said 'Let's start this group'.

The director of the video was called Willie Smax and he had a personality to match his name: a real eccentric, like a mad professor with big eyes, and all these dead good ideas. I liked him. It was shot in the same boxing gym where the Kray twins apparently used to train. I was pretty thrilled about that because I was intrigued by the whole Krays scenario.

J A S O N

I have a good memory of Robbie's cheeky grin at the end of the video and the funny bit where the girl walks past them and they both watch her.

M A R K

Jason The whole vibe of the single cover was much more relaxed than before – it's due to the clothes and the whole look.

Mark It was the first single artwork that tied in with the video and it worked very well.

Howard Of all of them so far this one really was a cool sleeve – the clothes we were wearing looked brilliant.

IT ONLY TAKES A MINUTE

Jason On the Corn Pops tour, because there was the theme of going back in time. We had some young kids who looked like each of us come on and perform the song while we had a coffee and a biscuit in the changing room. That was probably the best it's been performed, by some proper performers!

I LOVED IT WHEN WE PERFORMED THIS SONG WITH THE KIDS, A SORT OF A BREAK DANCE CHALLENGE. THE KIDS WERE ACE. I THINK BY THE END OF THE TOUR THEY WERE MORE POPULAR THAN WE WERE. **MO**

Howard When me and Jay wanted to make a dance routine I think it must have been on a bad day. We weren't really in the mood, so Jay just came down to my house. We don't always use dance rehearsal studios, we use houses, move furniture and do our routines in different rooms. He went in one room and I went in another and we just made up different bits and added them all together. So what you see is a mixture of those moves.

Mark We performed this in these kind of army trousers with big boots. It looked pretty funky if I may so say myself.

Jason We'd got our image together then: we sacked all the black leather, threw all that in the bin and were just dressing how we wanted to dress. We were just being cool and not worrying too much.

Howard I think it was me or Jay who had the idea for the puffa jackets with the TT on the back, track suit bottoms, trainers with buffalo laces. We thought it was a really good outfit, especially when the kids had matching outfits.

Gary When this got to be a hit, suddenly a lot of people found time to take an interest in us. They'd turn up everywhere with opinions about which trousers we should wear in Top Of The Pops. When you're stuck at Number 54 in the charts no one cares about your trousers.

Gary We'd talked very seriously about splitting up before It Only Takes A Minute came out. We wouldn't have been able to carry on if it had been a flop. You wouldn't believe how happy we were that it was a hit.

Mark We were doing a signing session in Tunstall when we heard that the single's midweek position was Number 16. We couldn't believe it. We ran out to see the fans and they were running up and down the streets screaming their heads off! I think they were even more pleased than we were. My family were over the moon. But I couldn't get through to them on the phone for about an hour because so many people were ringing my house to congratulate me.

A BIT SOULFUL, THIS ONE, WHICH GAVE US THE CHANCE TO TRY OUT A FEW MOTOWN MOVES, ALTHOUGH WE WERE DISAPPOINTED WITH HOW IT PERFORMED IN THE CHARTS.

I found heaven

Music & lyrics **IAN LEVINE AND BILLY GRIFFIN**   Lead vocal **ROBBIE AND GARY**   Release date **AUGUST 1992**   Highest UK position **15**

Howard This is probably, well definitely, my least favourite of the songs we've done.

Gary By the time we finished the Take That And Party album it wasn't the best single we could have released. At the time I Found Heaven was really the best one we had to hand.

Mark The arrangement was good with Rob and Gary taking turns on the lead line, and some great brass parts, but if I was honest it was never one of my favourite songs.

Jason I liked this tune: nice, catchy. It was more soulful than anything we'd done before: I like that better than the techno stuff. It got to Number 15 which is very respectable of course, but we wanted it to go higher because It Only Takes A Minute got into the top ten.

Gary Rob nearly sang the whole lead vocal on this one. We did changeovers: he did a verse and then I did a bridge and so on. Ian Levine was the producer - he has gone on to produce many fabulous groups like Bad Boys Inc. He had three big Dulux-type dogs and one of them decided to have a poo on the studio floor. Guess who stepped straight in it? Robbie Williams!

Mark Working with Ian Levine we encountered a vocal teacher called Billy Griffin. He taught us a lot and the nice harmonies were starting to appear.

Jason We did the video on the Isle of Wight. We wanted to go to Barbados to film it but we weren't very big then. We had a helicopter flying around and filming us dancing on the beach. We tried to make it look like we were actually in heaven - and that it was warm and we were happy. It was freezing cold actually, but it looks dead warm because of the special effects the cameramen used.

Howard A lot of people probably thought it was somewhere exotic. I think we lied for ages that we went somewhere far away. After the shoot we had a race between the camera crew and the artists and we were all running from one part of the beach to another. We legged it and little Marky with his Staffs legs won the race and I came second...You can see that on the video.

THE COVER FOR THE SINGLE WASN'T BAD - WE SHOT IT ON THE SAME DAY AS THE COVER FOR THE TAKE THAT AND PARTY ALBUM. I WASN'T SURE ABOUT THE HALO OVER MY HEAD...VERY STRANGE. **MO**

I F O U N D H E A V E N

I F O U N D H E A V E N

Jason As the song was quite soulful we decided to get a little bit soulful with the moves. So we watched a few Drifters videos and the old Four Tops and we tried to inject that into the routines. There was a point in the chorus where we have our hands in the air as if we're in close contact with heaven and that was beautiful.

Howard We tended to cool down the routine on this song. It wasn't the kind of song where you could do really funky and energetic moves. Some of the more relaxed and chilled moves, like a small spin, can look cool in a certain part of the song.

ON THE TAKE THAT AND PARTY TOUR WE DID A MEDLEY WITH SOME OF THE OLD MOTOWN SONGS. IT WAS BRILLIANT: WE ALL HAD THESE PURPLE JACKETS ON AND TOOK TURNS SINGING, WITH JASON ROUNDING OFF THE MEDLEY DOING I FEEL GOOD BY JAMES BROWN **MO**

Mark We did Top Of The Pops in these checked trousers: we looked like five Rupert the Bears.

Howard In the Motown medley we all looked very smart unless a few of us hadn't tucked our shirts in properly before we came through the curtain.

I THINK ABOUT ROB WHEN I HEAR THIS SONG. OUR ROBBIE, BECAUSE HE HAD QUITE A MAJOR PART ON THE TRACK AND I THOUGHT THAT REALLY BROUGHT HIS VOICE TO ITS FULL POTENTIAL – HE SANG IT NICE AND SOULFULLY. AND IT REMINDS ME OF HIM. JO

Mark Rob and Gary used to sing some naughty lyrics to this song, but I don't think I should repeat them. They were on the bit 'Then you came into my life'. All I can say is that they rhyme with the lyrics.

Gary There was no particular move forward with this single: it was a very average release for us. Luckily we released A Million Love Songs next which did us a good job. I don't think I Found Heaven did us any favours at all.

THIS IS A VERY SPECIAL SONG FOR US, A SMOOTH, GROWN-UP BALLAD WE'D PERFORMED A LOT BEFORE RELEASE. IT CHANGED OUR DIRECTION, AND BROUGHT US OUR SECOND TOP TEN HIT.

a million love  songs

Music & lyrics **GARY BARLOW** Lead vocal **GARY** Release date **SEPTEMBER 1992** Highest UK position **7**

Gary The slushiest song I've ever written. I wrote it in my childhood home when I lived with my Mum and Dad. I was fifteen or sixteen. The message is that I've written love song after love song in my life, but I still can't say 'I love you'. Sad really.

Howard That was a demo tape from years ago: I think Gary wrote it when he was sixteen years old, something like that. I was amazed how good the song was even before it was given to any producers. In the early days I wasn't really into listening to lyrics, but with this song you can't help listening to them.

Mark This was the first song we did that my Mum liked and so I was happy. She still says it's one of her favourites.

I WAS IN OUR MANAGER NIGEL'S OFFICE AND GARY SANG IT FOR ME, ACTUALLY SANG IT WITHOUT A PIANO, WITHOUT ANY MUSICAL INSTRUMENTS, IN THE BACK ROOM. A SUPERB SONG: I THINK HOW TALENTED GARY IS BECAUSE HE WROTE THIS WHILE HE WAS A WEE CHILD. I HAVE A PICTURE IN MY MIND OF GARY SITTING AT HIS PIANO IN SOLACE.

Howard Because this was a ballad and quite simple, the vocals had to be done more softly than on a lot of the other songs we'd sung.

Jason The backing vocals were quite difficult. They took a lot of time to get right: we wanted it to be so right. I think Gary sang the lead vocal in one take. He just waited until quite late at night when his voice was really warm and coarse - or is it hoarse? - and he did a superb job of the lead vox.

I loved this video shoot because there was no dance routine so it was simple and easy to make. There was loads of lovely food...the caterers did a really good job, perfect, lovely grub.

J A S O N

THIS WAS MEANT TO BE A STORY WITH ME AND THE BOYS IN CARTOON FORM, BUT IT DIDN'T REALLY WORK OUT, AND SO IT'S JUST A VERY SIMPLE BLACK AND WHITE PERFORMANCE VIDEO. MO

G A R Y

Somebody came up with the idea of a cartoon-style drawing. I couldn't get to grips with the idea initially. They filmed us and then drew over it with a brush. It sounded good to me, 'cos I thought 'Oh, they can probably touch me up in a few places'. But it was awful, so we went back to the black and white footage they'd filmed at the same time. We looked good but it wasn't quite what we expected it to be.

Jason I was going through a phase when I'd have a skinhead, sometimes a Mohican, a bit of a wild phase for me, but it used to itch and I never got any girls so I had to shave it. Just after this song was released I had a complete overhaul, grew my hair back, had a bit of a shave and began to look like a normal human being. So I remember not liking my own picture on the single artwork for this song.

Mark Quite eye-catching with all the little pictures of us in black and white.

WE PLAYED THIS SONG LOOKING QUITE CASUAL IN JEANS 'N' THAT. MY MUM SAW LIONEL RICHIE ON TV AROUND THE TIME AND SHE SAID 'WHY CAN'T YOU WEAR SUITS LIKE HIM?', SO THE NEXT TIME WE DID. (MO)

A   M I L L I O N   L O V E   S O N G S

Jason Without a dance routine, we always had a nice rest. I loved performing it on the Corn Pops Tour because I played guitar, and on the Nobody Else tour we actually got a fan out of the audience each night and sang it to her personally.

Mark During the live show we used to break the song down and do a singing bit with the crowd. Rob and me would do a kind of can-can behind the other boys while they were playing but one night they turned round and saw us... And after that we just did it with our big toes.

Howard I suppose in a lot of the gigs we did we used to make each other laugh because we were so close to each other, standing there with the microphones. Jay was always a good person to make laugh because once he was laughing he wouldn't stop.

THIS WAS THE SONG THAT MADE
EVERYBODY TURN TO ONE SIDE
AND SAY 'MAYBE TAKE THAT ARE
NOT JUST THIS POP BAND'. WE
PROVED THAT WE COULD WRITE
GOOD SONGS AND SING THEM
WELL AND TOUR LIVE. GB

Howard I remember performing this with Gary, both of us
playing the piano. That was a great experience for me. I
thoroughly enjoyed playing at the side of such a good musician.
In the early days some of the new clubs would announce us on
stage and get our name wrong like Take Five or Take This,
playing A Million Roses Later - some of the stupid titles they
gave the song always made Gary laugh.

Mark On the EP version I sang a lead vocal for the first time,
well half of one. Me and Gaz took a verse each on a song called
How Can It Be and my Dad's playing the guitar (bit of a plug
there, Dad).

Put your head against my life
What do you hear
A million words just trying to make
the love song of the year
Close your eyes but don't forget
what you have heard
A man who's trying to say
three words
The words that make me scared

A million love songs later
And here I am trying to tell you
that I care
A million love songs later
And here I am
A million love songs later
And here I am

Looking to the future now
This is what I see
A million chances pass me by
A million chances to hold you
Take me back, take me back
To where I used to be
And hide away from all my truths
through the light I see

Chorus

Feel for you baby, feel for you baby
A million love songs later and here
I am

ENERGY, THIS IS A SONG ALL ABOUT ENERGY AND THE CROWD

BOUNCING ALONG. WE NEVER EXPECTED TO HAVE SUCH A SUCCESS

WITH THIS SONG: NUMBER 3 OVER CHRISTMAS. BRILLIANT.

could it be

Music & lyrics **BARRY MANILOW AND ADRIENNE ANDERSON**   Lead vocal **ROBBIE**   Release date **DECEMBER 1992**   Highest UK position **3**

magic

IT HAD REAL ENERGY, REAL

ENERGY AND ROBBIE SANG IT REALLY WELL.

I WAS IMPRESSED WITH ROBBIE'S VOCAL.

Mark Of the two versions - the first on the earlier copies of Take That And Party and the actual single version - I feel the single version is much stronger.

Jason On Could It Be Magic, it's always the videos that spring to mind. This song was full of energy. I flipping loved it.

Howard I heard the Rapino Brothers' mix in a Previa van on the way to the Fridge in Brixton and it was brilliant. I thought 'Everyone's going to like this version. This is good'.

Gary This was a good song to cover. You can tell because it was originally a slow song and Donna Summer did it as an uptempo disco version and we did it as a Motown version, so it's an excellent song to cover.

Mark I had to go back in the studio to do some new vocals for the single, and Robbie had to do a new lead. On that particular day he was in fine voice: I think he got it in one go.

Howard Robbie's voice suited the song so well. I think we all had a go at it but I don't think anyone's voice suited it better than Robbie's.

Gary Two crazy guys called the Rapino Brothers did a brilliant job on it: it sounds so different from anything else. On the album we had a faster version of the song and in the end we re-pressed the album with their mix on it because it was so much better.

HOWARD

A girl wrote to Jim'll Fix It and wanted to be in one of the videos: she was in right at the beginning where she switched the light off in her garage and walked out. Then hey presto we'd appear. All we were doing was just freestyle, dancing on cars, in cars, and singing a song. No particular story line or theme. They asked if me and Marky wanted to go on Jim'll Fix It and I'd always wanted to meet Jimmy Savile because I used to try to do impressions of him. It was good to meet him, not that I said much, because I hardly say anything in interviews anyway.

GARY

The video was good fun. Rob was singing lead vocals and did a good performance, so I tried to stay out of the way as much as I could. It was only a one day shoot which I always like because there's nothing worse than shooting videos, I hate it.

MARK

The location was in this old aircraft-type hangar and we made it look like a garage. It was mainly a performance video with us all challenging for the camera. Jason was really ill on this shoot, although you can't tell when you watch it.

THE VIDEO WAS BIG FOR ME. I HAD A BAD KNEE THAT DAY AND I COULDN'T REALLY DANCE THAT WELL. WE WERE DOING A TOUR NOT LONG AFTER THAT AND I WANTED TO GET BETTER, SO I DID A LOT OF SITTING OUT AND WATCHING THE OTHER BOYS. WE HAD A COUPLE OF FANS WHO'D WON A COMPETITION COME DOWN AND STAR ON THE VIDEO. JO

IT'S JUST US BEING OURSELVES AND NOT TRYING TO BE SOMETHING THAT WE'RE NOT.

Mark We did a good shot for the sleeve of this single with The Face magazine where myself and the boys all wore T-shirts with each other's pictures on them.

COULD IT BE MAGIC COULD IT BE MAGIC

Jason I used to love performing this. The routine wasn't all that brilliant but it just had such energy and always got the crowd bouncing about, especially as our band are really tight. They kicked it and Rob got the crowd going. All the fans learnt the routine and would do it in the aisles - just amazing to watch.

Howard The dance routine live is hard on the knees. You can come to a part where you're so tired and you have to do Could It Be Magic and you know your knees won't take anymore. We could have done without putting that part in the routine.

Mark I liked the way we did this on the Corn Pops tour when we were all in baker boy outfits and it became a bit of a glitzy, jazzy song with us all running up and down the steps and clicking our fingers. The routine was set by Howard and Jason. There was this bit in the middle where we all stand behind each other and rock from side to side, but with me being the smallest I got to be at the front, so I think this was my fave bit, my five minutes of fame.

Mark This is a song that has been with us since the first ever tour, so there have been a few different outfits, from vests and loose pants to a sort of Romeo and Juliet look on the Everything Changes tour to some glitzy jackets and PVC trousers with sunglasses on the Nobody Else tour... Very confusing.

Jason I liked the outfit because it was just jeans and leather waistcoats and they're chilled, dressing down rather than up, establishing ourselves as the 'boys next door' doing a pop star bit. It worked, I think so anyway.

Howard On one of the tours we decided to wear nice linens, all very natural colours, beiges and creams. Nice and cool: with the routine being quite energetic it needs to be loose fitting.

Mark I knew we were becoming famous because even my local pub at the time used to play this song - it was a great Christmas present being Number 3 all over Christmas.

Jason Barry Manilow came to the concert in Manchester and then performed at the Apollo Theatre. He wrote the song originally of course, and he shouted out in the audience 'Does anybody know Take That?' There were a few claps and cheers and a few dogs barking, then this young lad who was supposed to be Robbie came out and he was singing and dancing like Robbie, and Barry did the performance uptempo like our version not his ballad style. I thought 'That's great, old Bazza doing it for the boys'.

THIS SONG IS ONE THAT WE ALL LOVE. WE GOT SO CLOSE TO THAT NUMBER 1 POSITION WITH THIS LAST RELEASE OFF TAKE THAT AND PARTY, BUT WE MUSTN'T BE TOO GREEDY.

Why can't I wake up with you

Music & lyrics **GARY BARLOW**   Lead vocal **GARY**   Release date **FEBRUARY 1993**   Highest UK position **2**

Howard Although I love the slow version, I do actually prefer the remix version... And this is one of my favourite songs. In fact it could be the favourite song of Take That.

Gary I've just checked back on my old tapes and I wrote this song in 1988, so this is quite an old song - it's a funky tune and I think you'll find it's one of Howard's favourites: I like this one too.

Mark Loved it. It was and still is one of my favourite songs. I think it was one of the first swing beat style songs to be heard commercially in England.

Jason I think it's one of our best tunes. I loved the ballad version and round about this time I started to learn guitar because I wanted to learn the tune. It got me more interested in the musical side because I'd come into the group mainly as the dancer.

Howard For the re-mix version we were in London for quite a few days and from mid-day to something like 3.30 in the morning. It was one of the best times we had recording a song. At the same time I bought a camcorder and was just filming everything that they did.

Gary We all went into the studio at the same time, which was unusual for us, we actually stood in there, the five of us, singing together and I think the harmonies were like nothing else we'd done in the past. It was remixed by a fellow called Steve Jervier who went on to produce Pray, Love Ain't Here Anymore and Babe for us.

Mark We recorded this down in London with the Jervier brothers. They had a pool table and a fab catering department. One big happy family, a really nice atmosphere.

Jason The recording was very demanding for me, probably easy for the boys. Nice vibe when we came to record this one.

WE FILMED THE VIDEO IN THIS MASSIVE MANSION WITH A MOAT IN JANUARY - IT WAS THE FIRST JOB WE DID IN THAT NEW YEAR. THE POOR MOAT WAS FROZEN OVER AND WE HAD THE FIRST TASTE OF GRAND HOTEL ROOMS. I WASN'T TOO KEEN ON DOING MY SHOWER SCENE, BUT IN THE END IT DID LOOK GOOD. BELIEVE IT OR NOT I'M NOT TOO COMFORTABLE WITH ALWAYS SHOWING MY BODY AND I HATE THE TAG 'THE BODY OF THE BAND'. 🅗🅓

J A S O N

I took a couple of souvenirs because we were getting a bit popular and I thought 'I'm going to take these souvenirs home' because I was a bit of a fan of Take That! Sounds a bit daft, really. I took the actual letter I'm reading in the video, it was our song written in French. I've still got it. I like things like that, you know, I'll keep them and show my children.

We shot the video in a chateau in France, a lovely place, full of antiques. Nigel, our manager, was running around telling us to be careful and not break any jars or that, or else we'd be paying the bills! The other thing was that all we could eat for three days was cheese and salmon. One night we thought we'd treat ourselves and go to a restaurant nearby, only to find when we got there that all they'd got on the menu was cheese and salmon...

M A R K

THE SINGLE ARTWORK WAS PRETTY NICE WITH THE FIVE OF US STANDING IN THE RIGHT HAND CORNER LOOKING QUITE RELAXED.

WHY CAN'T I WAKE UP WITH YOU

Howard On a lot of the tours we usually pair off to sing it and on the Berlin show we did I sang with Marky. I always have a little giggle when I look at him because when I'm sharing the microphone with him I'm near enough on my knees, poor little Marky. One of our best performances was for Top Of The Pops, but we were actually in New York so we did a satellite link. I don't know whether it was because we were in New York for the first time but I was buzzing, really happy with the way I was looking.

WE USED TO DO THIS SONG A CAPPELLA FOR A LOT OF THE TV SHOWS IN EUROPE. ONCE WE GOT THE GIGGLES AND THE DIRECTOR OF THE SHOW KEPT SHOUTING AT US BUT WE JUST COULDN'T STOP. IT TOOK US ABOUT FIVE MINUTES TO GET OUR BREATH BACK AND WE ALL HAD STOMACH CRAMP FOR DAYS. THE DANCE ROUTINE WAS PRETTY LAID BACK, JUST A FEW BODY WRIGGLES AND THINGS... OOO ER, VERY SEXY!

Jason The dance routine was quite mellow. I couldn't decide whether to make it mellow or funked up because we'd done the two versions of the song. As it happens we settled for sort of in between, swaying a bit with the music and then getting funky on the middle eight.

Mark I remember some T-shirts the fans had made for us saying 'Why did I wake up with you'. I thought to myself 'Charming that, ain't it!'

Howard On the video shoot we went down for one meal and before we all went down we had to see who could dress up as the best train spotter, the naffest between me, Mark, Gary, Jenny Turner, the make-up artist, and Jay. Guess who won. Jay.

Can't decide if I should read or
think
I'll keep an open mind, 'til the day
sets in
Hear you thinking
Hope you hear me thinking too

Why can't I wake up with you
So you're there when I open my
eyes
Baby, why can't I wake up with
you. You're my life

Feel alive, so I'll just begin
To rest my mind, before you ring
me
Hear you call me, I'm so willing to
call back
Hear you thinking
Hope you hear me thinking too

Chorus

So good to be near you
So dark when you walk from my
side
Baby why can't I wake up with you
You're my life, you're my life

THIS WAS THE BIG ONE FOR US: OUR FIRST EVER NUMBER 1 RECORD. THAT GAVE US SUCH A HUGE BUZZ... IT'S A FEELING THAT NEVER REALLY WEARS OFF.

PRAY

Music & lyrics **GARY BARLOW**   Lead vocal **GARY**   Release date **JULY 1993**   Highest UK position **1**

Gary I think we knew when we finished recording this song that we had something special. Monster hookline, monster chorus. I think we were more confident about this record than anything else we'd ever recorded.

Howard By this time Gary had that much technology in his studio even his demos were sounding like master recordings. But he stills plays all the demos to us before we all decide whether a song should be released. And again we just loved it. It had such a catchy chorus.

Mark The first time I heard Pray was in the studio. I loved the song. It sounded kinda gospelly with the choir at the end, but I still can't work out what the sound is right at the beginning, whether it's water or talking...

Jason It had a controversial edge to it. If it's got that 'pray' word in it, people can hook into it as deep as they want. It reminded me of a Madonna tune in a way, and I'm a big fan of Madonna so I like it for that reason. And I just thought 'Yeah, hit' straight away – bang. Dead excited.

Jason We used a producer called Steve Jervier and we were all excited to be working with him because we knew he was good. It was the first time I think that when we came to do the vocals somebody in the studio was there, aiding us, helping us, not actually singing but doing vocal arrangements. It was such an improvement on other tunes, a whole lot more sophisticated. We were definitely moving up in the world.

Mark We had a vocal arranger called Mark Beswick who used to make us all do vocal exercises before we started singing, but we used to just laugh at each other.

Howard We always have a good time with the Jervier brothers in their studio. They're a good laugh. We also had the vocal producer there so the recording probably took us longer because we were always laughing and we'd have to go into the corners and face the wall to do our vocal warm-up.

WE HAD GOOD FUN RECORDING PRAY. WE PUT A GOSPEL CHOIR ON THE RECORD, AND BRASS. STEVE JERVIER PRODUCED THE RECORD: THIS WAS THE TIME WHEN WE WERE STARTING TO USE NAME PRODUCERS. GB

The video was filmed in Acapulco so we were starting to spend a bit of money on the videos!

GARY

This will always be a good memory as we travelled afar to Mexico... This video was a ball, we were just lapping it up. One thing that sticks out in my mind is that we were short of gospel singers at the end so we had a few of the crew in the line-up. We actually got James, one of our security guys, in the line-up and if you look at the end of the video you can see him singing it, well, trying to sing it... He didn't know all the words and I don't think any of the others knew them as well.

HOWARD

We did a lot of individual shots: mine were in the sand and I just had to keep making shapes and things. I love the shot where Rob rubs his eyes and then the tears fall down the girl's face and also where Jason holds the mirror reflecting the sun. Gary always goes on about his end shot where the camera pulls away. He used to say 'Watch this shot, watch this shot'. Other memories: playing football on the beach with the locals, and the fact that there were black pigs everywhere. Honest.

MARK

MARVELLOUS, BECAUSE WE'D REACHED THAT POINT IN OUR CAREER WHERE THE RECORD COMPANY WOULD TAKE US TO A NICE COUNTRY. IT WAS FLIPPING GREAT, DEAD HOT AND SUNNY AND WE ALL GOT BURNT. ACTUALLY I GOT DEHYDRATED AND HAD TO BE TAKEN TO THE DOCTOR'S BECAUSE I'D BEEN SITTING OUTSIDE IN THE SUNSHINE READING SCRIPTS AND I FORGOT TO DRINK ANY WATER.

Mark This was a group one shot in Acapulco - we all have burnt faces from too much sun, but it doesn't look too bad.

Jason I loved it, loved it, beautiful.

Howard There were two formats for this single – both taken in Acapulco on the beach – and we were all nice and brown and healthy. Yeah, very good.

P R A Y • P R A Y • P R A Y • P R A Y • P R A Y

Gary We were in tour rehearsals for our first arena tour at the time the single was out, so of course Pray was in the set. I think the Pray routine is one of the best we've got. Very simple, very slick.

Jason One of the best routines so far. Howard and I choreographed this one: I think Howard had more to do with this one. He got all creative for this song, did a great job, and I just added the little frilly bits in the middle. The whole routine really helped bring the song to its full potential.

Mark I love the performance of Pray on the Everything Changes tour best, where we are all in the black cloaks. It is very eerie and sets the song up well, but nearly every night when we took the cloaks off, one of us couldn't get it right. It was really funny: you could feel the others laughing at you...

Howard There was this move where I had to lift Mark up. I used to have to put my head between his legs and throw him and collapse on the ground. A few times we couldn't get it right and we were always laughing our heads off. With nearly all of our faces covered none of the crowd could see who was in which outfit and we'd be circling round the stage in a figure of eight, not knowing where we were going, bumping into each other and crying our eyes out.

When the time gets near for me to
show my love
The longer I stayed away for
Hiding from a word I need to
hear now
Don't think I'll hear it again
But the nights were always warm
with you
Holding you right by my side
Right by my side
But the morning always comes
too soon
Before I even close my eyes

All I do each night is pray
Hoping that I'll be a part of you
again some day
All I do each night is think
Of the times I closed the door
to keep my love within

If you can't forgive the past I'll
understand that
Can't understand why I did this
to you
And all of the days and nights
OK I'll regret it
I never showed you my love
But the nights were always warm
with you
Holding you right by my side
But the morning always comes
too soon
Before I even close my eyes

Chorus

Surely we must be in sight
Of the dream we long to live
We long to live
If you stop and close your eyes
You'll picture me inside
I'm so cold and all alone

Straight on back to me

Chorus

Mark This song allows for many different scenes with outfits, although I don't think we've taken this song to its potential yet. I still love the black cloaks best.

Jason Excellent outfits. One time we came out as sort of monks, dressed all in black, and then the next time we came out dressed in white, trying to be angels. None of us are angels, but we were trying our best to look like them.

Howard I think every outfit has been brilliant, whether we've been in white or black.

Mark We were travelling from our homes to a place in Wales to rehearse for our Take That And Party tour when we first heard that Pray was number one. It was amazing. I taped the charts and used to listen back to the DJ saying '...And this week at Number 1 is Take That with Pray'. I've still got the tape somewhere.

Jason I just think Number 1 straight away, bang, first ever Number 1.

Howard I remember listening to Capital Radio. Foxy, a top DJ, was on and he put Pray on and said this was one of his favourite records of the year and that made me chuffed. It's good to hear that off a radio DJ.

Gary We proved the people who doubted us wrong. Just when they thought we were at our end, here we were coming back with a Number 1 record. This for me was the real start of a five piece group: we were all so involved in everything we did for this record.

THIS IS A HUGE AUDIENCE FAVOURITE.

A REAL UP-TEMPO VIBE: ALL YOU CAN SEE IS THE WHOLE PLACE

BOUNCING UP AND DOWN. AND WE GOT THE CHANCE TO WORK

WITH MISS LULU AND HER RED HAIR. FAB VOICE.

relight my fire

Music & lyrics **DAN HARTMAN**   Lead vocal **GARY**   Release date **SEPTEMBER 1993**   Highest UK position **1**

Mark I love the original version – I used to dance to it in the clubs on a Friday and Saturday night, and so I enjoyed recording this one very much.

Howard To be honest I heard the version by Dan Hartman in the dance clubs a long time before we actually started recording it, and I thought 'It's going to take a lot to beat this version'.

Jason I can't remember where I was when I first heard the track, but my first impressions were great. I couldn't wait to meet Lulu, I really couldn't wait. My elder brother Simon fancies her and when I told him she was on our track he was dead jealous.

Gary It was a good idea to use Lulu. I knew when I met Lulu that she wasn't just going to be someone I'd work with once and that would be the end of it. I knew that we were going to be friends for a long time because she's such a lovely woman.

Gary Originally Robbie was going to sing this record, but when we went into the studio, it didn't actually suit his voice... The day Lulu came into the recording studio, she sang so well, and I went in and did a few backing vocals with her too. It was an excellent day. There are so many different pieces to this record, so many different backing vocals and stuff like that, it seemed to take forever to make this record.

Howard This song whizzed by when we actually recorded it. It was as simple as this: we went into a recording studio in London, did our vocals – I know I did mine separate to Lulu – on the chorus, because there wasn't much in the verse, and then we were out of there, finished.

Mark At some point we had Mark Beswick in to do vocal arrangements, but in the end we recorded it with a guy called Joey Negro. I can just remember him speaking in a really mellow voice saying 'It's a bit flat, man!' The song didn't really come to life until Lulu got her vocals down. She turned up with a flask of tea.

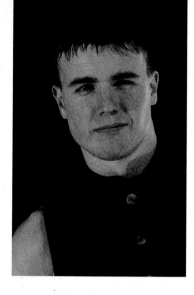

GARY

It's got a bit of a risqué side to it: lots of transvestites and Jason in the shower with this girl. It was a big move on for us. I think it was one of our only records that crossed over to the clubs.

JASON

During the daytime the club was free for us to use. We had all these weird people come in dressed in weird clothes: one man dressed just like a big red fat monster, transvestites, lots of lovely young ladies, although you couldn't tell because they all had too much make-up on. A very freaky sort of video. We always perform better in the videos if we have a bit of an audience there.

WE SHOT IT AT THE MINISTRY OF SOUND IN LONDON AND BASICALLY JUST HAD TO DANCE FOR A DAY. THERE WERE LOTS OF DIFFERENT CHARACTERS IN THE VIDEO: MY FAVOURITE WAS THE RED BALLOON MAN. MY T-SHIRT SAYING 'JUNKIE'S BADDY POWDER' CAUSED AN UPSET WITH THE TV PEOPLE BECAUSE THEY THOUGHT IT WAS A BAD INFLUENCE. (MO)

HOWARD

I like it - it's a good video. Everyone was dressed up to the eyeballs in lots of colourful costumes. It was amazing actually doing a video with Lulu, who's been in the business a lot longer than we have.

IT WAS VERY PRETTY, BUT IT DIDN'T REALLY GO WITH THE MOOD OF THE SONG. WE'RE ALL WEARING NICE CARDIGANS AND THINGS – I LOOK LIKE BING CROSBY. **MO**

RELIGHT MY FIRE • RELIGHT MY FIRE

Jason Great to perform this live because Lulu would often be with us. She'd come bursting out at the end and do her little bit and we'd go 'Yeah!' I choreographed the first verse, Howard did the second and I did the chorus; we also had the help of Kim Gavin. It's a fast routine, funked up, man, it's bang on. It was around this time all these other boy bands started coming out of the woodwork - no disrespect to anybody else, but we had to show them who was the best.

Howard The performance that sticks out in my mind is from the last tour when there were just the four of us. It was nerve-wracking and very strange to be coming out for the first time as a foursome. But we did an excellent performance and showed we could still do it. The routine was quite hard to piece together. Me and Jay did it: some of the moves are quite complicated, one of the hardest for the lads to learn. We actually had to teach the professionally trained dancers.

Mark One night when we were doing a performance in Sheffield, I had this beige leather outfit on and it split. Not just a little split - my bum was hanging out of the trousers! I think that's where Howard got the idea to show his on the Corn Pops Tour. It is quite a difficult routine to do, especially wearing four inch platforms. There was also a bit where we had to spring up from our backs to our feet and it used to be a sight watching us all trying to do that.

Gary We play Relight My Fire on every tour, it's such a good song to play live. It gave us the chance to do a brilliant dance routine... As usual I wasn't included that much.

Jason On the tour before last we dressed as fun devils and it was brilliant. We had this fella, this one man in the whole of the UK going to the press saying we were devil worshipping and it wasn't fair and he wasn't taking his daughters there... We couldn't believe it - it was a bit of fun and a little bit cheeky, Howard showing his bum cheeks off. Lulu had this big wig on and she was very scary. When she was dressed as a devil she frightened me so I wasn't going to worship **her.**

Gary The title of the song means we can always think of something outrageous to do to it, like wearing devil costumes or using fireworks on stage. It's all relative to the title, but we were lucky to find that particular song because it's perfect for us.

Howard How can we forget the colourful skirt knitted by my Gran with the dead sheep on my back, the controversial chaps I wore where I'm showing my buttocks, and the gold pair of shorts which looked a bit like a mini-skirt and one of them doors that you walk through in the greengrocers with all the floppy coloured bits that blow in the wind.

Mark It made me laugh a lot when the stories were relating us to devil worshippers.

Howard We went over to do Relight My Fire in France, at Eurodisney. All the Disney characters were on stage with us, and Robbie sussed out that Mickey Mouse was actually a French woman. So we kept on pinching Mickey Mouse's bottom... She got a bit angry and swore at us in French.

Mark I kind of liked the picture of me on the bed on the Nobody Else tour where all the hands were coming through touching me, but I would, wouldn't I?

Jason I remember that bloke that moaned a lot. We'll take this moment to apologise to anyone we might have offended.

Gary Lulu's a total professional. She came out on tour with us, and we had to rehearse the routine. Despite all her years in the business she still went through it dozens of times to make sure she got it absolutely right.

THIS WAS AN IMPORTANT SONG FOR US. BABE WAS MARK'S FIRST LEAD VOCAL. THE STRONG STORYLINE

Gary I have to confess, it isn't about Mark. It's not about anyone I'm afraid. But I wish it was, because I always think it sounds good when people like George Michael say 'Oh, it happened to a friend of mine'.

Howard I think of little Marky, that he got to do his first lead vocal and made a very good job of it. Gary played us a demo, and it sounded a bit more like a story than a song. We thought it was excellent.

Jason I was dead pleased because it was the first song that Mark had ever sung lead vocals on. He got a chance to prove his vocal ability and he did a great, great job, all sincere and melancholy. The first time I heard it I was over the moon. One of the best, an absolutely beautiful song – the words set my hair on end.

BABE

Music & lyrics **GARY BARLOW**   Lead vocal **MARK**   Release date **DECEMBER 1993**   Highest UK position **1**

MADE FOR A GREAT VIDEO, AND IT WAS ALSO ONE OF OUR BREAKTHROUGH TRACKS IN EUROPE.

Gary The song was finished off in Japan. Mark was keen to do a lead vocal on something and Jason was learning the guitar at the time. There's only about four chords in this song so it was a perfect opportunity for Jason to learn the song all the way through. He and Mark had been rehearsing the song for about six months and I hadn't really finished it. I hadn't written the middle eight, and then I came up with the idea of this boy going home and seeing this girl who's had his baby.

MY FIRST MEMORY IS ME
AND JASON PRACTISING
THIS SONG TOGETHER
FOR MONTHS WITH
GUITAR AND VOCAL. I WAS
SO NERVOUS WHEN I HAD
TO DO MY FIRST LEAD. **MO**

Mark I thought 'Does my voice really sound like that?' The first version was really nice, but for the single I went back into the studio and did a new lead which was much better. This was our first encounter with a man called Chris Porter. I went to his studio with Gary full of cold and Chris's wife made me this magic drink with ginger and lemon which really cleared it up.

Jason When Mark started singing it, this was the time I was just getting a few chords going on the guitar. I got Gary to write out the chords and I got going. Beautiful. Just right.

Howard With this song being a ballad it had to be sung more softly, a little bit more carefully. Mark did a brilliant job. He's a perfectionist: he can be in the studio all night if he wants to be.

Gary Originally I recorded it with Mark at my house so we could present it to the record company. Then we had it remixed by Chris Porter, which was good because he went on to work with us on lots of other stuff after that, including Back For Good, The Day After Tomorrow and Hate on on Nobody Else.

HOWARD

We filmed it just off Canary Wharf in this disused factory. On the second day I was actually a bit ill and they were playing in the snow - well, the false snow. I couldn't play in it because I had a really bad chest. It was a very, very cold day. Besides that it was good fun filming, and I really wanted to keep that bicycle but they wouldn't let me.

HOWARD

I remember seeing the finished version. We were playing live at Wembley, ran onto the coach because it's got a video player on it and we had a few little tears in our eyes when we watched it. I think Gary had tears in his eyes because he couldn't stop laughing with me on that bike. He kept having to rewind it to have a good laugh.

I ARRIVED ON THE SHOOT AND HOWARD RODE PAST ON THIS BIKE, WEARING THESE SILLY OLD CLOTHES. I DON'T THINK MANY PEOPLE KNOW IT'S HIM, THEY THINK IT'S A WALK-ON, OR RIDE-ON. IT JUST TICKLED ME A BIT. **JO**

An excellent video, made by the same guy who did Pray, Greg Mazuak. I think it was brilliant.

GARY

I really enjoyed shooting the video because it was like acting at the same time. It took a couple of days on some moorland near London - my favourite shot is when Howard goes past on his bike.

MARK

THESE WERE LIKE PICTURE FRAME VERSIONS OF THE SINGLE - THE CLOTHES WERE QUITE CASUAL.

B A B E • B A B E • B A B E • B A B E • B A B E

Gary Babe is a good one to do on tour because there is a story to it, and we're always able to do something different with it. On the Corn Pops tour we used like an interactive technique when we all came walking out through the screen. It was a good song to include that on.

Mark My first ever performance of Babe was in Bournemouth and it was very emotional. I was filling up inside. The crowd pretty much sang the song for me - it was beautiful.

Jason I loved it because I really got to play on this one - the first song I ever played on-stage guitar. I was so nervous, I'd practised and practised and practised. I learnt the song, but then all the chords changed to suit Mark's voice on tour. So I had to learn the whole thing again, but I pulled it off. Oh god, I was so scared though, I really was so scared.

Howard We all like performing Babe live because it gives us a bit of a breather and it's a good song to sing. The most perfect bit for me is the little boy playing with his toy and running up the stairs through the screen and then Mark picking him up. That's what you call perfect timing. But some nights he didn't get it right, bless him. To be honest I would probably prefer Mark to do it on his own. It just feels as if it's his song. But that's my little opinion.

Howard On the last tour we did in '95, that was a brilliant outfit. The dancers, the violinists and the costume that Mark was in. I think Marky picked that one actually: he's a very good clothes stylist.

Mark We can wear anything really for this song – we did a 3D special Top Of The Pops and for that performance we wore the same as the video.

Jason We kind of stuck with the theme of the video when we came to perform the song live. A real second-hand look, the old dressed down, worn look. The lights down low and a very moving, moody song to perform.

Mark Gaz does a country and western version of the song – I'll get him to do it for you sometime.

Jason Gary gave me these chords and the lyrics and I was practising them on the beach in Miami. We were on a promotional tour over there. I was learning the song on the sand and this lovely young lady approached me. I thought 'Hang on a minute, I'm in here.' And she sat down next to me and said 'What are you doing?' I said 'I'm just learning this song.' She was nice company. About half an hour later these friends of hers came up to us. She stood up and said 'Look everyone, look at the song he's just written'. And it just clicked: she thought I'd written the whole song. I was going to say 'No', but I was too embarrassed and just went along with it. I was dreading the other lads coming up on the beach and finding out what had gone on. I didn't write it at all. I've never written a song. And that's that.

Gary Babe wasn't number one at Christmas like we expected it to be. Mr Bloody Blobby knocked us off the top, but we don't mind about that too much.

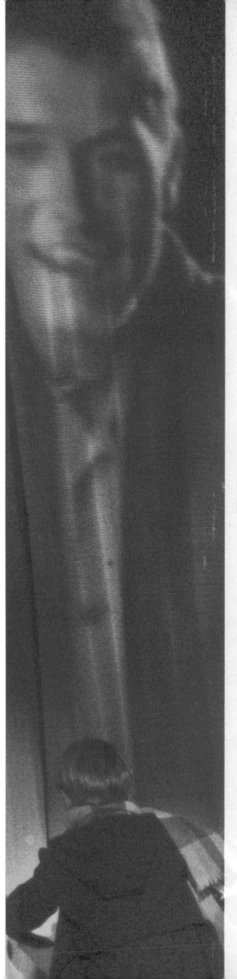

I come to your door
to see you again
But where you once stood
Was an old man instead
I asked where you'd be
He said "She's moved on, you see
All I have is a number
You'd better ask her not me"

So I picked up the phone
And dialled your number
Not sure to put it down or speak
And then a voice I once knew
Answered in a sweet voice
She said "hello"
Then paused before I began
to speak

Babe, I'm here again
I tell you I'm here again
Where have you been?
Babe, I'm back again
I tell you I'm back again
Where have you been?

You held your voice well
There were tears I could tell
But where were you now?
Was you gonna tell me in time?
Just give me a town
And I'll be straight down
I've got so much to tell you
About where I have been

As I walk down your road
Can't wait to be near you
Can't keep this feeling in inside
As I stand at your door
You answer in a sweet voice
You said "hello"
Then pause before I begin
to speak

Chorus

As I looked away, I saw a face
behind you
A little boy stood at your door
And when I looked again
I saw his face was shining
He had my eyes, he had my smile

Baby I'm back again
I'm back again
Babe where have you been
Babe, please take me back
Take me back home again
Baby I'm back again
I'm back again
Babe I'm here for you
Babe just me and you
You and me

Chorus

HAVING THREE STRAIGHT NUMBER ONES WAS BRILLIANT, BUT THEN TO GO OUT AND DO IT FOUR TIMES IN A ROW WAS ABSOLUTELY MIND-BLOWING.

Everything Changes

Music & lyrics **GARY BARLOW, MIKE WARD, ELIOT KENNEDY AND CARY BAYLIS**   Lead vocal **ROBBIE**   Release date **MARCH 1994**   Highest UK position **1**

Gary A bit of history about the writing of this song: I don't think Robbie had a lead vocal on the album. It was like 'God, we have to write something for Rob quickly because he's not going to be happy at all.' We went into the studio in Sheffield - we were working with a couple of guys who did Wasting My Time with us. And I said 'We need to write something for Robbie'. So we wrote Everything Changes.

Howard We were in the studio in Sheffield recording something else, and the song just came up as an idea. That simple. I liked it: it seemed like a very jolly song.

Mark I was worried about the release of this song. For some reason I thought it wasn't going to be a hit. Proves what I know, doesn't it? I used to like Rob's talking at the beginning - it made me laugh.

Jason I always thought this was a great pop song, and it suited Robbie's voice perfectly.

Gary Rob came into the studio the night we wrote the song, loved it, did an excellent vocal. He really enjoyed doing it. What was good - which doesn't usually happen - is that the mix that was on the album actually went out as the single mix. So that just proves we couldn't improve on what we'd already done.

Mark We recorded it in Sheffield with a bunch of guys called Five Boys - they produced Wasting My Time and Whatever You Do To Me as well. It was good recording there, because it meant we could go home when we'd finished!

Jason When we were recording Everything Changes I used to enjoy watching the expressions on Robbie's face when he had to sing the intro 'Forever more...' It was kinda high for him.

Howard It only took Robbie a few times to get his vocal right. As far as the backing vocals went, they were just straightforward, very simple.

HOWARD

The video was filmed under a railway arch in London. While we were filming it I wasn't so sure how it was going to turn out, but I was really happy with it. At the end of the day we all had good fun on the shoot.

THERE WAS A LITTLE BOY ON THE VIDEO SHOOT WHO PRETTY MUCH STOLE THE SHOW. HE WAS DANCING NON-STOP ALL DAY. IT'S A NICE VIDEO WITH LOTS GOING ON. NOT SURE OF THOSE NAILS THOUGH. **MO**

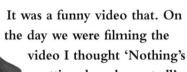

It was a funny video that. On the day we were filming the video I thought 'Nothing's getting done here at all' because it just didn't feel like we were getting anything on camera. Then when I watched the video back I realised that Rob had done a brilliant performance on the video and everyone looked like they were having a good time. So it turned out really well in the end.

GARY

JASON

Whenever I think about this video, the first thing that comes into my head is Gary, sitting on the piano, with his cheesy smile. And that little boy was dead funky. He was only about seven but he out-danced the lot of us.

Mark I don't think this is one of our better single covers. We're all stood in tie-dyed T-shirts against a blue background and we look ill.

Howard To be honest I don't like this single cover, especially the photograph of me, or the clothes.

BEFORE THIS PHOTO

SHOOT, I'D ALWAYS HAD SHORT HAIR,

BUT I GREW IT LONGER FOR THIS ONE,

AND PEOPLE SEEMED TO LIKE IT.

EVERYTHING CHANGES • EVERYTHING CHANGES

Mark This is an easy song to perform live because all the moves are round mike stands, so it can be set up anywhere. I remember Rob running from one side to the other, standing on the speakers and putting the security into a panic. There was also a move that didn't get into the final routine that involved a kind of skipping with no rope. Gaz used to do it all the time; he kept saying 'I've got this one' and you'd see him skipping off into the distance.

Howard Robbie forgot the words a few times, but that wasn't unusual for him! I'm not too keen on this particular routine to be honest, although it's enjoyable to do. When you're rehearsing for a tour, it's hard to make the time to do a dance routine.

Jason Live, the keyboard player and Robbie would always race each other through the introduction to the song – Robbie usually won.

Gary We did a live link for Top Of The Pops from Rotterdam and we were absolutely knackered that day. We had to do this link before the main show that night, but it came across pretty well on the old Top Of The Pops.

THE BEST OUTFITS WERE ON THE NOBODY ELSE TOUR IN THE PVC AND SILVER SHIRTS. WE'VE NEVER REALLY EXPERIMENTED WITH THIS SONG COSTUME-WISE. **MO**

Howard The worst fashion disaster for us was we did Top Of The Pops and we asked for these clothes a week before. We described what we wanted and they kind of got the wrong ones. We were wearing these bell-bottom flares with tight T-shorts. I didn't get the approval off my family, and I'm sure the others didn't either.

Howard: I never really saw myself singing the lead on this song, and me and Gary actually sang it on the last tour - which was a surprise.

Mark On the last night of the Everything Changes tour during the dance break of this song, me, How, Jay and Rob just stopped and watched Gary do it. It was so funny - he just looked at us, shook his head at us and carried on whilst we were all applauding.

Jason: For some reason, when we performed this song, the lyrics started to change on their own, so a phrase like 'Everything changes but you' would slowly turn into 'Everything changes ahoo!!'

Gary The single was backed by a medley of Beatles songs, but we weren't comparing Take That with them, although we do have something in common: they were a band who had fun and that's what we've always tried to do.

Girl, come over here
Let me hold you for a little while
And remember I'll always love you
For ever more
Everything changes but you

We've said goodbye
The taxi cab is waiting
Now don't you cry
Just one more kiss
Before I have to go

Hey girl I know
The situation changed
And so much is new
But something in my life
Remains the same

'Cos everything changes but you
We're a thousand miles apart
But you know I love you
Everything changes but you
You know every single day
I'll be thinking about you

The rumour's true
You know that there've been others
What can I do
I tell you baby
They don't mean a thing

Now girl don't go
And throw our love away
I'll be home soon
Back in your arms
To hear you say that
Everything changes but you

We're a thousand miles apart
But you know I love you
Everything changes but you
You know every single day
I'll be thinking about you

Everything changes but you
We're a thousand miles apart
But I still love you
Everything changes but you
I spend every single day
Thinking about you

Though everything changes around us
(Baby don't you cry)
We will be the same as before
For ever more

Everything changes but you
We're a thousand miles apart
And I still miss you baby
Everything changes but you
You know every single day
I'll be thinking 'bout you

Everything changes but you
I'll be thinking about you
Thinking about you
Everything changes but you
Cos you know I love you
Know that I love you.

THIS WAS THE LAST SONG RELEASED OFF THE EVERYTHING CHANGES ALBUM. WE'D HAD FOUR CONSECUTIVE ENTRIES AT NUMBER 1 BEFORE THIS SONG - AND THEN WE FOUND WET WET WET SITTING AT THE TOP ALL SUMMER WITH LOVE IS ALL AROUND.

Love ain't here anymore

Music & lyrics **GARY BARLOW**   Lead vocal **GARY**   Release date **JUNE 1994**   Highest UK position **3**

Jason I didn't think we should release it, but I'm not one of those 'I told you so' people. I mean Number 3 - brilliant, very respectable, but we wanted another Number 1 because we were used to them by then. We weren't too frustrated though. I like Wet Wet Wet - their drummer is a dude - and they deserve the success they received for that song.

Mark I always like the ballads, and this is a strong vocal song. If anything it's a little sad. 'Love ain't here anymore'.... Boo-hoo.

Mark I don't really remember much about recording this song. It was produced with the Jervier brothers around the time of the recording of Babe, so I probably had my mind on other things.

Howard I remember thinking while we were recording the video 'Hey, this is going to be a wicked video', but when I saw the finished result I was a little bit disappointed.

Mark The video was supposed to look quite arty. We sort of stole the idea from Madonna's Rain video, although at the end of the day it doesn't quite have the same effect. I love the bit with the orchestra. It looks like a massive room, but it's actually a painting on glass that was shot with the orchestra in the background. Overall: good idea but it didn't come to life properly.

Jason I wasn't keen on this video. I have liked most of our videos much more than the other lads – I think we've got some cracking videos – but this one I didn't like. I think we turn out just too pretty. In the Rain video Madonna's eyes are dead big and her cheeks are dead clear, but ours didn't come over like that, perhaps because we didn't have Madonna's money to spend on it.

VERY MATURE. WE LOOK

KIND OF SOPHISTICATED

BUT A LITTLE BIT PENSIVE.

I DO LIKE THAT. **JO**

Mark We all looked very smart on the cover with our suits and that. It was a nice black and white sleeve, although somebody commented on me looking like the lead singer of Suede. I took it as a compliment!

L O V E   A I N ' T   H E R E   A N Y M O R E

Mark I liked the bit on the Corn Pops tour where we all sat on the front of the stage: it looked nice and relaxed. Step one two, step one two again. The most difficult thing was remembering when to advance and when to sit down: even we aren't that thick. Well, we got it right most nights!

Mark This should be a get the suits out song although on tour there was no time for a change, so we did it in knee-length boots, checked trousers and white shirts. Not quite what I had in mind. It could have been worse. At least we managed to find a spot to take the skirts off. Confused, are you? So was I.

Howard All the clothes were great – especially being in white.

Mark It would have been funny if one of us had got pulled into the crowd and ravished, but unfortunately these things don't seem to happen at our concerts. Well, maybe next time, eh!

Jason I remember us having jokes in the van about there not being a crowd to watch us perform at this gig we were going to... And we said we should sing 'The Crowd Ain't Here Anymore'. It was much funnier than that at the time...

Baby, don't you want me to go
So honey, why don't you beg me to stay for love
And talk the way we used to talk
Till we both know what we've lost
Never say the words we did before
When it was over

Love ain't here anymore
Love ain't here anymore
It's gone away
To a town called yesterday
Love ain't here anymore

Listen, oh listen, I don't wanna let go
So maybe we can change the way we feel for love
And open up the way we did before
Now is the right time and I'm sure
You'd never say the words you did before
When it was over

Chorus

And when I find a place for me to keep my sweet love
Then I will leave it there forever more
And when I find someone to share I'll never give up
I will hold and believe that this life leads to more

Chorus

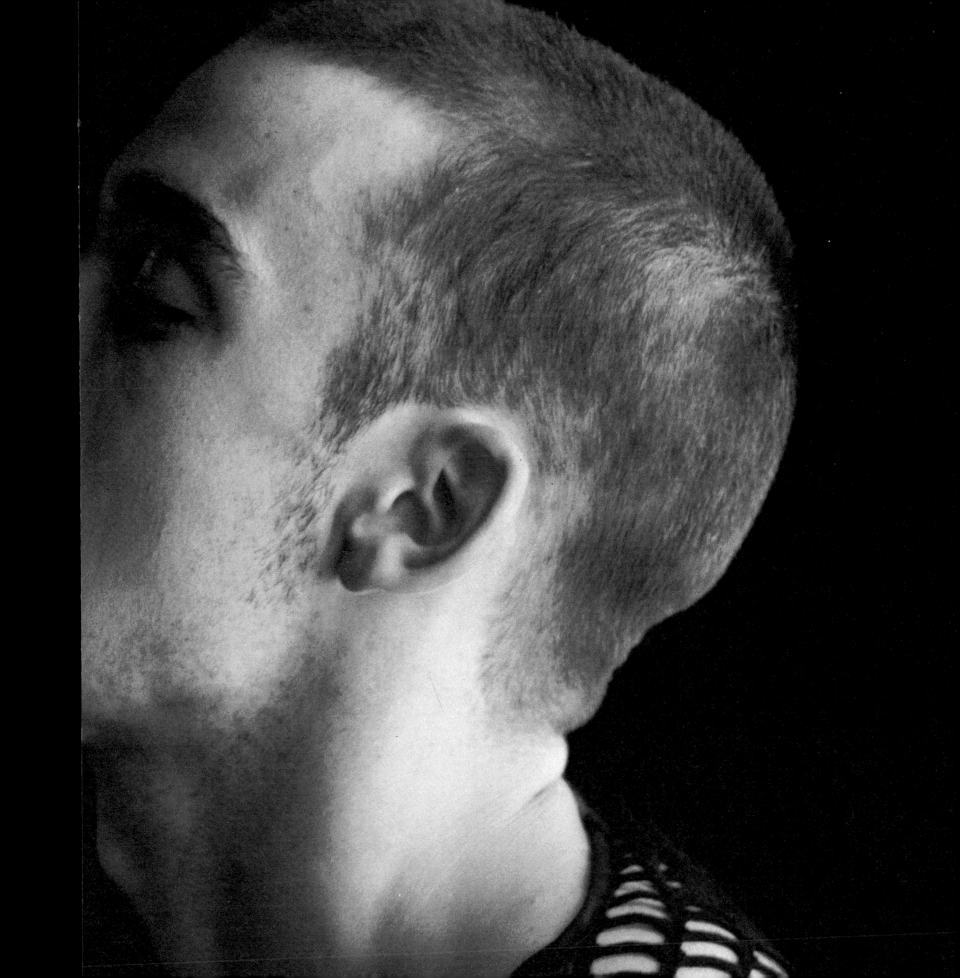

WE ALL KNEW AS SOON AS WE HEARD IT THAT THIS WOULD BE OUR FIRST SINGLE OFF THE NOBODY ELSE ALBUM. IT'S GOT A GREAT FUNKY ROUTINE, AND ON THE VIDEO WE TRIED OUR HANDS AT A LITTLE BIT OF ACTING. SEE YA AT THE OSCARS!

Music & lyrics **GARY BARLOW, MARK OWEN AND ROBBIE WILLIIAMS**   Lead vocal **GARY**   Release date **OCTOBER 1994**   Highest UK position **1**

Howard Gary was in my studio showing me around a few new things I'd just bought and he played this little chorus bit on the piano and started to sing 'Sure'... and that was the beginning of the song. A few days later he'd already done his demo, and it was brilliant.

Gary I remember playing this song to the guys while we were on tour in Belgium at a piano in the bar. And it was literally just an old piano. I was singing 'Sure, so sure' and they all liked it. They all said 'Oh, I think that's going to be a good record for us, that.'

Jason The first thing this song makes me think of is all of my good friends, because I invited them to my flat one night. We had something to eat and drink and I played them the demo. I said 'Lads, what do you think?' and they loved it. That buzzed me, because I knew if my friends liked it then it stood a chance in the charts. My Mum likes every song, you know what I mean, she's a bit biased like.

Mark I first heard Sure when we were driving round in a van in Korea listening to Gary's demos and deciding which ones we liked. I thought it was a pretty funky number. I liked the way it started with just the piano part before the drums kicked in. When we were rehearsing for the Corn Pops tour Gary said to me and Rob 'Go and write a middle eight', so about thirty minutes later we came back and said 'We've done it'. I think we surprised ourselves with that one.

Mark We'd started to use Gary's studio for the main part of the recording. We did this song with the Brothers in Rhythm. The hardest part was remembering the words for the middle eight, the 'holdin', squeezin', touchin' ' bit because silly boy here forgot to bring them from my home.

THE SONG STOOD OUT BECAUSE IT
WAS A VERY UNUSUAL MELODY.
GARY SINGS IT SO WELL. HE SINGS
IT WITH VENOM, MAN. IT WAS
FUNNY AND WICKED – BRILLIANT.
IT WAS A GOOD DAY FOR
RECORDING THAT DAY. IT WAS
COOL, REAL COOL. **JO**

Howard Recording this song was very relaxing because we only had to travel up to Gary's house and record in his studio. We raided all his biscuits, drank all his coffee and just chilled out all day.

Gary The Brothers in Rhythm were really good producers and they set about doing a version of Sure. They put a really funky beat behind it and we all came in again, at my house this was, stood round the mike and sang all the answer lines. It was an exciting change for us because it was a different type of music than we'd ever done before, a bit harder, a bit tougher.

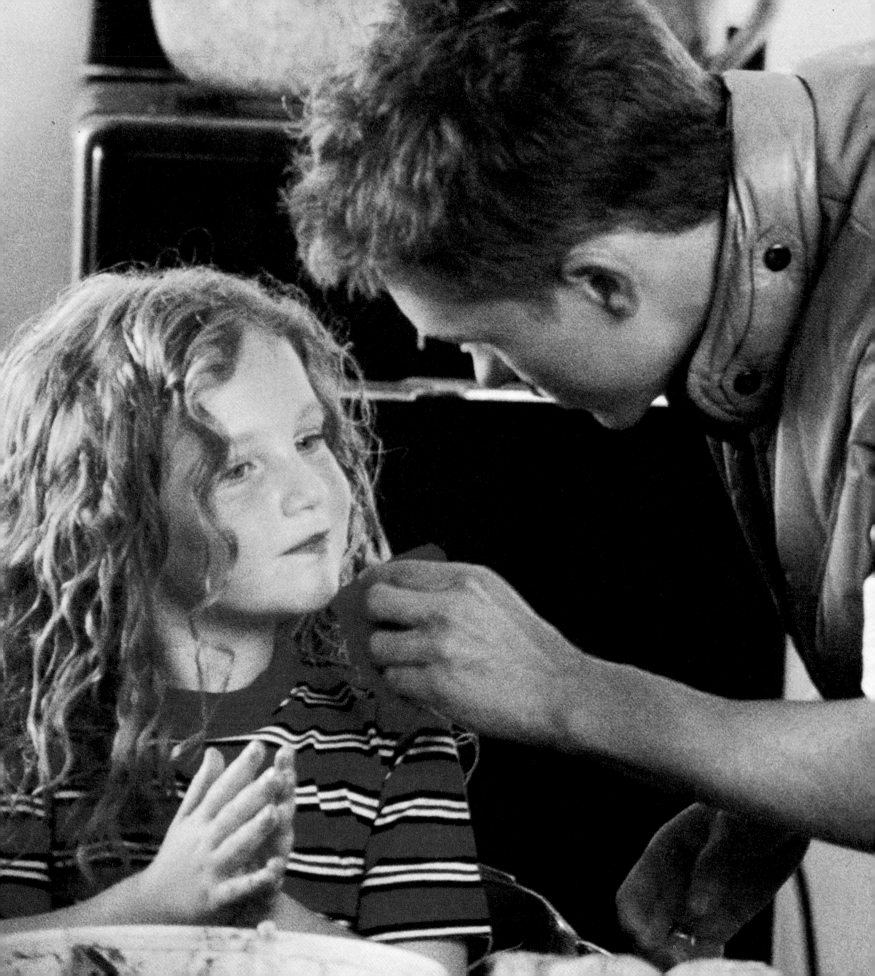

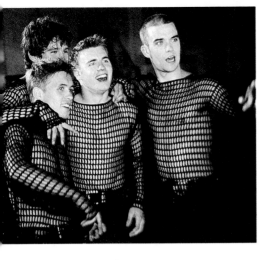

G A R Y

It was a weird day because everyone came dressed in this certain style, with their hair slicked back and all the make-up on. It looked like the Relight My Fire video again, so we made everybody change, get all the gunge out of their hair and look dead natural. There was a bit of confusion, but it all came together in the end.

M A R K

The bit of acting at the beginning made me realise how difficult it must be to make films. It took two days, one for the acting, and the other for the dancing and party scene. A great video to do, lots going on, and the little girl was lovely.

WE DECIDED WE WERE GOING TO DO SOMETHING A LITTLE DIFFERENT, A BIT OF ACTING. YOU KNOW, HOW OLD JACKO DOES ON THRILLER. IT TURNED OUT WELL AND MARK'S A RIGHT LITTLE ACTOR, A NATURAL BEFORE THAT CAMERA, BUT I DIDN'T GET ENOUGH TALKING PARTS. THE WHOLE SHOOT WASN'T LIKE WORKING, IT WAS LIKE GOING OUT TO A DISCO.

H O W A R D

I had only just had my eyebrow pierced. This very kind Japanese woman who did our make-up was cleaning my eyebrow every two minutes because she could see it was swelling up. When we arrived in the morning there were lots of models, dancers and extras there and they were all in the wrong kind of clothes, so we had to desperately phone someone up and change them into something more suitable.

Mark There were two covers: on one all our faces are against a black background which looked very strong, and the other more casual one had us in the clothes we wore for the video.

Howard My favourite is the cover with five heads and a black background.

Jason Very hard and funky. It worked.

Gary A good record sleeve - this was a time when we had all changed our images, going for something new; it felt good and fresh.

S U R E • S U R E • S U R E • S U R E

Jason I love performing this song live. We were going to bring another choreographer into this routine. But then me and Howard said 'We'll have a go at this, we like this song'. And then I think we did the best routine we've done to date together. It's a very hard song and we had to do a hard funky sort of routine - it really, really belts out.

Gary When we perform this one live it's always the one that the audience does the answers to. It's very easy to sing along to this song which probably makes it attractive.

Howard We did a performance of Sure at the end of '95 in America - it was weird to be actually performing in front of an American audience, and surprising that we had a few fans there as well. The routine was more R&B and when we were making up the moves it came very easily. I think my favourite move is at the beginning of the first verse - 'I'm sitting here waiting for my lover'...

Mark On the Nobody Else tour we performed this song with two Thunderbird cars on stage. On one occasion where I jumped onto the car, I missed and fell flat on my face. I don't know what was worse, the pain of falling or the embarrassment as everyone was laughing at me. It was my own fault: I was getting a little cocky with those cars anyway.

Jason Usually we have the black look for this, funky black or army pants, which really suits the song.

Howard I liked the black net tops we wore for the video shoot. I wish we could have worn them on stage for the live show but instead we used the tops for Give Good Feeling - we do like to spread our coppers about!

Mark On the Corn Pops tour we performed this song in T-shirts with black and grey trousers, knee-length boots and a wrap-around skirt, similar to the video. It looked pretty good. On the Nobody Else tour we all had silver grey outfits on while the girls who were dancing with us wore red. That was a strong image.

Jason When Howard and I put the routine together, we were practising it in a marquee. We had it perfect and then our manager came in: he had to video the routine so he could send it off to a television programme, and when it came to the crucial point, dead proud, we just made a right cock-up of it. And little Mark got stung by a wasp, so he had to drop out half way through - we were a shambles.

Howard I was once looking out of my hotel window and saw about twenty-five girls on the pavement about ten floors below and they were all doing the Sure dance routine. Some of them weren't doing it right, so I felt like going down and tidying it up a bit, but then I thought it wasn't such a good idea...

Mark When we first heard it I remember us saying we sound a little Chinese on the chorus. If you listen you'll know what I mean.

I'm sitting here writing to my lover
Last time we met I wasn't so sure
Now I'm hoping, maybe dreaming,
for a life as one
When she reads this I'm hoping
she'll call
But I need more much more than
before
I need positive reactions whenever
I'm down

I'm sure so sure
It's heaven knocking at my door
Sure so sure, so come on inside
Need you so much
More and more each time we touch
Sure so sure that it's sweet love I've
found

It's not a game so don't play
hard to get
There's no connections holding us
down
Isn't it a shame that it never happened,
oh yeah
Though still here we are the second
time round

It's gotta be social, compatible, sexual,
irresistible
It's gotta be right for life

Chorus

Holdin', squeezin', touchin', teasin',
Wantin', wishin', waiting, thinking
of you love, yeah yeah
Grinding, grooving, feel it moving
Binding, breathing, 'bracing, breeding
With you girl

It's gotta be social, compatible, sexual,
irresistible
It's gotta be right for life

Chorus

THIS SONG, WHICH WAS OUR FIRST EVER HIT IN THE

STATES, ALWAYS GETS THE CROWDS SINGING THEIR

HEADS OFF. IT'S GREAT FOR US TO SIT AND LISTEN.

MAYBE WE SHOULD PAY TO GO TO *THEIR* CONCERT NEXT TIME!

BACK FOR GOOD

Music & lyrics **GARY BARLOW**   Lead vocal **GARY**   Release date **MARCH 1995**   Highest UK position **1**

Mark The strings and guitar stood out for me initially. It's a really catchy song and there was a bit of a buzz for it. I was originally going to do a lead vocal on this one, but my voice wasn't really suited to it, so up stepped MR GARY BARLOW.

Jason I can't say too many good things about this song. We were all really happy with it. A classic, classic song. I wish we could write fifty just like it. I was at Gary's studio and Mark was singing this and it sounded beautiful.

Howard America - that's what this song reminds me of. It got to Number 7 in the charts there, which is amazing.

Gary I wrote Back For Good at the same time as The Day After Tomorrow. It was very easy to write, I wrote it in about fifteen minutes I think - and that was with a coffee break! The songs I write quickest turn out the best.

Howard On some songs when you have to go back to another vocal part you get sick of hearing it in your earphones. With this song I didn't get bored at all. It's one of those songs where you can just listen to it all day and still not get bored.

Gary We had two months at my house doing the backing tracks to the song. Mark was going to sing the lead - he'd done numerous vocals on it - and one day I was just getting a level on the mike and started singing 'Back for good...' Chris Porter, the producer, said 'You should really have a go at singing it, because it sounds so good'. That's where the idea came from for Mark to do The Day After Tomorrow, which actually suits his voice much better than Back For Good.

Jason We recorded it together all round one mike. All five of us round one mike doing the BVs, the backing vocals. It was just a good laugh. I'd got my new car and used to drive up to Gary's every day in this soft top. Good memories... Nice hot days.

Mark Vocals for this as well as the production were done at Chris Porter's studio. We stayed over at his house for about a week and at the same time did Hate It, The Day After Tomorrow and Nobody Else. Nice and relaxed, with a little waiting area upstairs where MTV played all day.

M A R K

Getting cold and wet, we shot it at Pinewood Studios in London. We had rain machines everywhere. It was a fun video to shoot, though we were just dancing around and playing in the rain like little children.

H O W A R D

I remember being sat in a trailer for half a day and hoping it was going to get warm. The good part of the day was driving one of those customised American cars around: yes, ladies and gentlemen, I was the one that drove it. Another memory was watching Robbie when we were having water poured on our heads. With him having a bald head it was much more painful, and when the scene had finished he was in agony. If you have a close look at the video you can see the pain beginning, just before the video ends.

NIGHTMARE VIDEO SHOOT.

FREEZING. WE GOT RAINED ON.

IT WAS STUDIO RAIN. WE CREATED

IT OURSELVES, GOD KNOWS WHY.

I THINK WE ALL CAUGHT COLDS AND WE WERE

GOING ON TOUR NOT LONG AFTER. BUT DEAD

PLEASED WITH THE VIDEO. **JO**

A very uncomfortable sort of video. I was doing nothing but complaining on the day, but I actually think it's our best video. In the States it's not often they take the same videos we use in England. Usually it will be improved or they'll have a different idea, but for Back For Good they used the same one.

G A R Y

Mark A group shot with us all in these satin suits against a corrugated metal background. Mixed opinions: some days I like it, some I don't.

I LOOK A BIT DODGY, AS IF I'VE JUST SNEAKED IN THE BACKGROUND AND HAD MY PHOTOGRAPH TAKEN WITH FOUR STARS. HD

BACK FOR GOOD • BACK FOR GOOD

Howard The day after the charts came out, we were performing at Wembley and it was so good to announce that we were at Number 1. Every night I had to drive the American car on stage perfectly (I do actually drive the car) and park it carefully over this trapdoor, so the others could come up through the boot. If you're even ten centimetres off the line it stops them getting up, and a few nights I had to just keep going backwards and forwards to get it right.

Gary Back For Good's always good to perform live because Jason can play guitar and I can play piano on it. I really feel as if I'm singing my heart out when I do this song. It's quite hard to sing: there are a lot of high notes in it so I always get a bit nervous if we've got to do live vocals on TV.

Jason In America we performed Back For Good live on the radio with just myself on the guitar and the four vocals. It was beautiful – I don't mind saying so myself – I was buzzing.

Mark This is probably our most successful song to date, so it goes down well pretty much everywhere. I like it when we do a cut down version with Gaz on keys and Jason on his guitar. We played this song outside the Rockefeller Center in New York at 8 in the morning for a TV show. That was pretty amazing – it rained then as well!

Mark We don't really have a set outfit or look for this song - I still think it looks nicest when we smarten up a little.

CLOTHES HAVE ALWAYS BEEN IMPORTANT IN OUR CAREER. IN THE EARLY DAYS IT WAS 'DRESS TO IMPRESS', NOW WE'RE DRESSING MORE INDIVIDUALLY, HOW EACH OF US WANTS TO DRESS. WE TRY TO BE IN HARMONY BUT WE ALSO TRY TO INVENT OUR INDIVIDUALISM. WE DO IT WELL WITH THIS SONG BECAUSE THERE'S NO DANCE ROUTINE.

Jason We were on the David Letterman show, the biggest show in America, and that was one hell of a buzz. We also had to perform this song in front of our record company in America and that was very nerve-wracking. We walked into this quiet room, and everyone was dead silent, a few smiling faces but some stern looks because they've seen it all before, all types of acts and bands. So we had something big to prove. There's Gary on piano, myself on guitar and the four vocals and we pulled it off. That was mint, that was.

Gary We went to Abbey Road studios - where the Beatles recorded their albums - to record the strings. Instead of walking into the control room I went straight into the string room and they all went wrong! I said 'Sorry!' but I stood in there for a bit and the sound was amazing... I thought 'That's my song, that'. Thirty-two people playing my song.

I guess now it's time for me to give up
I feel it's time
Got a picture of you beside me
Cot your lipstick mark still on your coffee cup
Got a fist of pure emotion, got a head of shattered dreams
Gotta leave it, gotta leave it all behind me

Whatever I said, whatever I did I didn't mean it
I just want you back for good
Whenever I'm wrong just tell me the song and I'll sing it
You'll be right and understood

Unaware but underlined I figured out this story
It wasn't good
Yet in a corner of my mind, I celebrated glory
But that was not to be
In the twist of separation you excelled at being free
Can't you find a little room inside for me

Chorus

And we'll be together, this time is forever
We'll be fighting yes forever we will be
So complete in our love we will never be uncovered again

Chorus

ONLY TWO WORDS, BUT THEY MEAN A LOT TO US.

IF YOU LISTEN TO THE LYRICS, THEY SAY IT ALL REALLY.

IT'S A SONG ABOUT THE LIFE OF TAKE THAT,

A SONG ABOUT US.

Never forget

Music & lyrics **GARY BARLOW**   Lead vocal **HOWARD**   Release date **JULY 1995**   Highest UK position **1**

Jason I loved the lyrics. They blew me away because previously Gary had mainly written about love and relationships. This one has a big, big message and I loved it for that reason. I think we had a more direct influence on Gary writing this song.

Mark When I first heard it – the early version at Gary's house, and the mix travelling to France in the back of a car – I thought it sounded huge, with the choir and everything.

Gary When I played the boys Never Forget they were all quite excited. I'm a real love song writer really, and I think everyone was a little bit relieved that at last I'd written something that wasn't related to love. It was talking about our past, very simple lyrics about where we'd been and where we'd got to. That we're never going to forget where we've come from and all the things that mean so much to us.

Howard When Gary does his demos he brings them along in the van. He puts them on and he always says 'Right...' When it came to Never Forget he said 'Pay attention to the lyrics'.

THE RECORDING OF THE SONG
WENT BRILLIANT. I'VE NEVER HAD
ANY DOUBT IN HOWARD'S VOCAL
ABILITY. HE'S NOT THE MOST
CONFIDENT OF CHAPS, BUT HE'S GOT
A SUPERB EAR FOR MUSIC: HE
NEVER GOES OUT OF TUNE AND HE
CAN PICK HARMONIES OUT OF THE
AIR JUST LIKE THAT. IT'S NICE FOR
HIM TO COME FORWARD AND SHINE.
HE IS MY HERO IS HOWIE!! **JO**

Howard It did take longer because I was singing
it. Gary came to me and he said 'Listen, Doug, this
is one for you', which made me very happy and it
took me a very, very long day in London. It was a
hard song to sing and I remember playing everyone
the demo with my vocal on and they all thought it
was wicked.

Mark This was initially recorded with Brothers in
Rhythm for the album and it had a kind of spacey,
dreamy start to it. We went to do some extra vocals
at the studios, some individual lines and just a few
extra backing vocals to thicken it up. Then Jim
Steinman got his hands on it and it came back
sounding unbelievable.

Gary We had it remixed by a fellow called Jim
Steinman who's done all the Meatloaf albums. I was
flabbergasted when it came back from his studio in
America because it just sounded enormous, and
he'd said to me on the phone a week earlier 'I'm
not going to do too much to it'. And he hadn't
really, he'd just added a full horn section and a full
boys choir and made the song about eight minutes
long. So I'm glad he hadn't been on the phone
saying he was going to do a **lot** to it!

M A R K   O W E N

M A R K

We wanted to try and get across what has happened for us in Take That, a kind of fly on the wall view of the last few years. I actually helped to edit this video which was a new experience for me: I remember trailing down to London with about twelve videos under my arm taken from our camcorders and some poor sod had to sieve through it all for the best shots.

H O W A R D

Well, we had lots of different other ideas for the video but it came at the right time, I suppose. It's quite moving to see all the bits.

WE HAD THIS CAMERA CREW OUT ON THE ROAD WITH US IN EUROPE; WE DIDN'T HAVE A VIDEO SHOOT AS SUCH. I LOVE IT BECAUSE IT'S GOT US WHEN WE WERE YOUNGER, GROWING UP. I'VE WATCHED IT A THOUSAND TIMES BECAUSE THERE'S A MILLION MEMORIES. **JO**

G A R Y

This video shows the five of us as real good mates getting on well. I think that comes across, and everyone enjoys watching it because you can see we're having such a good time and haven't got too serious about ourselves.

J A S O N

Mark The artwork was really clever with myself and the boys as children holding up a picture of us from the time - really, really, really clever.

Jason I loved the artwork for this. We all had to take pictures of ourselves from when we were kids into the office and it was brilliant. We were dead pleased, it was absolutely perfect.

Howard It's a good cover - as you can see on the front sleeve, I'm the ugliest child. It's not my fault, it's my Mum and Dad's fault. On the inside cover there's some wickets and grass. That was me playing cricket at Petercombe Park in Audenshaw, so for anyone that knows the place, get down and have a look.

N E V E R   F O R G E T • N E V E R   F O R G E T

Mark Our first performance of this song live was on the Nobody Else tour. Words cannot describe the feeling of looking off the stage and seeing a mass of hands being held in the air. An amazing finish to the concert and a great finish to the first five years of Take That.

Howard It was brilliant to perform as a live vocal, especially being the finale song. When Top Of The Pops came to record it at Earls Court, they had all the cameras around me and I sang the second verse and then the first verse. It totally baffled the crowd and messed up my whole show, but I had to take it as a bit of a laugh.

Gary Of course it's a fabulous song to sing live because it's so uplifting. We finished the Nobody Else tour with it, and everybody said that after the concert the people were going home with smiles on their faces. I think that's what this record does to you.

Jason Every time we've performed this song it's been marvellous. I love those big audiences: on the chorus of 'Never' there can be 20,000 pairs of hands in the air. I'll be bored with number ones, and sex, before I'm bored with that thrill. It's true you know!! We had a lot of problems with the routine: it warranted just a 'stand by the mike and perform it', but there was a real groove. We wanted to make this one mellow but funked up a bit and a we had a few disagreements... In the end it was just right, a few funky little moves and then the chorus – throwing our hands in the air and having a merry old time.

Jason Very mature, very grown up, very black jackets with white handkerchiefs coming out of the pocket and black slacks and shoes - a bit dressy. We look like we're going for dinner. On the last tour it was the last song, so we could finish and go straight to dinner without having to get changed - that was handy.

Mark We finished the Nobody Else tour with a string section and the choir all in white. We had the long black jackets. It looked very smart.

Howard We had long Donna Karan black coats, very suitable for a grown-up song. I felt very comfortable with it.

THERE WILL ALWAYS BE A BIT

OF SADNESS WITH THIS

SONG. IT WAS WRITTEN

ABOUT FIVE OF US AND NOW

THERE ARE ONLY FOUR. BUT

THE SHOW MUST GO ON.

Jason Never Forget was about our travels and had lots of positive messages, but it's got a bit of sadness about it because it was the last record we did with Robbie. It was ironic that we chose that song as a single and then Robbie left.

Howard I remember being on stage singing live and this girl just jumped on a chair, pulled her jumper up and pulled out her jugs. It was a bit of fun, because we were all looking at each other thinking 'What a pair!'

Been on this path of life for so long
Feel I've walked a thousand miles
Sometimes strolled hand in hand with love
Everybody's been there
With danger on my mind I would stand on the line of hope
I knew I could make it
Once I knew the boundaries I looked into the clouds and saw
My face in the moonlight
Just then I realised what a fool I could be
Just cause I look so high I don't have to see me
Finding a paradise wasn't easy but still
There's a road going down the other side of this hill

Never forget where you've come from
Never pretend that it's all real
Someday soon this will all be someone else's dream

Been safe from the arms of disappointment for so long
Feel each day we've come too far
Yet each day seems to make much more
Sure is good to be here
I understand the meaning of "I can't explain this feeling" now
It feels so unreal
At night I see the hand that reminds me of the stand I make
The fact of reality

Chorus

So don't ever think don't take for granted
That these good times are due to you
And don't ever believe all that you read
It's a game, a game you can win

Chorus

WE ALL LOVE THIS SONG, THE OLD BEE GEES NUMBER –
ANOTHER GREAT BAND FROM MANCHESTER! WE WERE
LOOKING FOR A FINAL RELEASE TO ROUND OFF THE GREATEST
HITS ALBUM, AND PICKED THIS ONE AS A SPECIAL THANK YOU
TO EVERYONE WHO'S EVER BOUGHT ONE OF OUR RECORDS.

How deep is your love

Music & lyrics **BARRY, ROBIN AND MAURICE GIBB**   Lead vocal **GARY**   Release date **FEBRUARY 1996**

Howard I was the one who came up with the idea of doing this song when we were suggesting possible cover versions for the new single: it's a classic, classic number – I remember it from the Saturday Night Fever soundtrack – and suited the kind of vocal arrangement we could give it.

Jason A brilliant, timeless song: as soon as I heard the backing track for our version of the single I said 'Yeah, that's the one.' Beautiful.

Gary We actually did a demo of this song a couple of years earlier, but it just didn't gel for some reason. Then when we were over in New York doing some promotion work, Howard suggested we should try it again and so when we got back we started work straightaway, and this time round everything fell into place.

Mark The first time I heard How Deep Is Your Love I was about fifteen – I'd probably heard it on the radio before that, but the actual time I can recall the song was when I bought one of those Greatest Love Songs compilations. A girl had just finished with me and I was a bit depressed... and then I depressed myself even more by listening to all these soft ballads.

Gary The whole recording for this song was done over at my house. You can't really improve on the original, so we kept the arrangement very simple, very straight, quite acoustic with those vocal harmonies and the Latin percussion feel. I heard that one of the Bee Gees - Barry, I think it was - said that he thought Back For Good was the best single released in America in the whole of '95, so this was our way of paying them a bit of a tribute.

Mark We went over to Gary's house with Chris Porter, who we've worked with before, and basically just put it together there. Gary had this new power generator that was sending out all this hissing which the mike was picking up, so whereas we all usually sit on his settee, we had to scrap that idea, and all sit on the floor, and lean the settee up against the hissing machine to hide the noise...

Howard The best thing about recording at Gary's house is that it's not far from where I live, so it doesn't involve having to go all the way down to London - and it makes everything so much more relaxing for us.

IT'S NOT ME ON THE GUITAR ON THIS TRACK, SADLY. THAT BREAK'S A BIT TOO GOOD FOR ME - I'LL JUST STICK TO THE OLD STRUMMING. **JO**

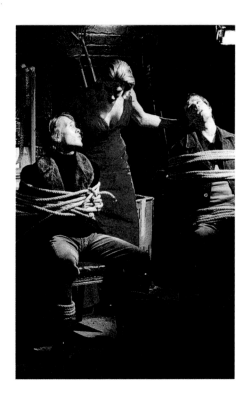

H O W   D E E P   I S   Y O U R   L O V E

Mark Strange, very strange. We wanted to do a video that wasn't really obvious for a ballad like How Deep. We didn't want to be walking along through the countryside - so the director came up with this great idea, a bit like a mixture of Misery and Silence Of The Lambs.

Gary Paula Hamilton plays this crazy woman who's kidnapped us all and kept us tied up in a cellar. Then she puts us in this van, still tied up, and drives us off to the edge of a cliff where she pushes one of us over. But the idea was that we didn't know who it will be so when they said one of us would go off the cliff, I thought I bet I'm going to draw the short straw - I usually do.

Jason You always think that when you meet a supermodel they're going to be really difficult, but Paula was tops, very easy to work with, very down to earth, and helped us get through two really long days of shooting.

Howard Before this I'd have thought that a whole day of doing dance routines would have been more tiring, but it's harder just sitting in a chair, not able to move. We were tied up in those chairs for hours, and you couldn't get out - it took too long to take all the gaffer tape off. I had this chair taped to my bum for like ten hours!

THIS WAS A SESSION WE DID OUT IN NEW YORK WITH PHILIP OLLERENSHAW, AND HE TOOK A WHOLE LOAD OF SHOTS OUTSIDE AND INSIDE THE STUDIO. THE SHOT WE USED ON THE SLEEVE IS VERY RELAXED: WE'RE JUST SITTING ON THE FLOOR. **MO**

Gary The key for me on this song are the vocals, just how far they've come on – how everybody's singing is much much stronger.

Mark When we first started off, we were travelling around in this yellow minibus and we used to do medleys of songs including a Queen medley and a Guns'n' Roses. They weren't serious medleys, they were just mucking about. We also did a Bee Gees medley and that's why we'd wanted to do How Deep for a long time. Howard and Rob used to do all the high bits, the rest of us couldn't get up there, we were just screaming in the high parts!

THE THATOGRAPHY

DO WHAT U LIKE
Words and music: Gary Barlow and Ray Hedges
Producer: Ray Hedges for Zyrus Productions
Additional production and mix: Graham Stack
UK release: July 1991 on Dance UK
12" b/w Waiting Around

Video director: Ro Newton and Angie Smith
Sleeve design: Artworks
Sleeve photography: Ian Lea

PROMISES
Words and music: Gary Barlow and Graham Stack
Producer: Pete Hammond
UK release: November 1991 on RCA
7", MC and 12" mixes b/w Do What U Like

Video director: Willie Smax

ONCE YOU'VE TASTED LOVE
Words and music: Gary Barlow
Producer: Duncan Bridgeman
Engineer: Matt Kemp
UK release: January 1992 on RCA
7", MC b/w Guess Who Tasted Love
12" picture disc Aural Mix b/w Guess Who Tasted Love (Guess Who Mix)/Once You've Tasted Love (Radio version)

Video director: James LeBon

IT ONLY TAKES A MINUTE
Words and music: Dennis Lambert and Brian Potter
Producer: Nigel Wright for Skratch Music Productions
Engineer: Robin Sellars
UK release: May 1992 on RCA
7", MC b/w Satisfied
Limited edition 7" b/w It Only Takes A Minute (Royal Rave Mix)/Satisfied
CD b/w I Can Make It/Never Want To Let You Go/It Only Takes A Minute (Deep Club Mix)

Video director: Willie Smax

I FOUND HEAVEN
Words and music: Ian Levine and Billy Griffin
Producers: Ian Levine and Billy Griffin
Arranged by: Ian Levine and Nigel Stock
UK release: August 1992 on RCA
7" limited edition picture disc, MC b/w I'm Out
7" poster bag b/w I Found Heaven (Mr F's Garage Remix)
CD b/w I'm Out/Promises (7" Radio Mix)/I Found Heaven (Classic 12" Mix)
Video director: Willie Smax

A MILLION LOVE SONGS
Words and music: Gary Barlow
Producers: Ian Levine and Billy Griffin
Arranged by: Ian Levine and Nigel Stock
UK release: September 1992 on RCA
7" with transfer tattoos, MC b/w A Million Love Songs (Lovers Mix)
EP 7" and CD b/w Still Can't Get Over You/How Can It Be/Don't Take Your Love

Video director: Brad Langford
Sleeve design: T&CP Associates
Sleeve photography: Peter Mac

COULD IT BE MAGIC
Words and music: Barry Manilow and Adrienne Anderson
Co-producers: Ian Levine and Billy Griffin/The Rapino Brothers
UK release: December 1992 on RCA
7", MC b/w Take That Radio Megamix
12" poster bag Deep In Rapino's Club Mix b/w Take That Club Megamix/Could It Be Magic (Mr F Mix)
CD Rapino Radio Mix/Deep In Rapino's Club Mix/Acappella/Ciao Baby Mix/Rapino Dun/Paparazzo Mix/Deep In Rapino's Dub/Club Rapino Mix

Video director: Saffie Ashtiany
Sleeve design: T&CP Associates
Sleeve photography: Kate Garner

WHY CAN'T I WAKE UP WITH YOU
Words and music: Gary Barlow
Producer: S&P Jervier
Engineer: Mark Franks
UK release: February 1993 on RCA
7", MC b/w Why Can't I Wake Up With You (Live version featuring acappella)/A Million Love Songs (Live)
7" b/w Promises (Live)/Clap Your Hands (Live)
CD b/w A Million Love Songs (Live)/Satisfied (Live)/Take That Medley/Why Can't I Wake Up With You (Live)

Video director: Liam Kan and Grant Hodgson
Sleeve design: T&CP Associates
Sleeve photography: James Martin

PRAY
Words and music: Gary Barlow
Producer: S&P Jervier and J Wales
Additional vocal production: Mark Beswick
Engineer: Pete Craigie
UK release: July 1993 on RCA
7" MC b/w Pray (Acappella)
CD1 Duo pack b/w Pray (Acappella)/Pray (Alternative Club Mix)
CD2 Club Swing Mix b/w It Only Takes A Minute (Tommy Musto Club Mix)/Once You've Tasted Love (Harding & Curnow Remix)

Video director: Greg Masuak
Sleeve design: T&CP Associates
Sleeve photography: Andre Lansel

RELIGHT MY FIRE
Words and music: Dan Hartman
Producers: Joey Negro and Andrew Livingstone for Z Productions
Additional vocal production: Mark Beswick
Engineer: Dixoid
UK release: September 1993
7" b/w Why Can't I Wake Up With You (Live)
MC b/w Why Can't I Wake Up With You
CD1 b/w Full Length Version/Late Night Mix/All Night Mix/Night Beats
CD2 b/w Why Can't I Wake Up With You (Live)/Motown Medley (Live)/Take That And Party (Live)

Video director: Jimmy Fletcher
Sleeve design: T&CP Associates
Sleeve photography: Dean Freeman

BABE
Words and music: Gary Barlow
Producer: S&P Jervier and J Wales
Additional vocal production: Mark Beswick
Engineer: Pete Craigie
UK release: December 1993 on RCA
7" picture frame sleeve, MC Return Remix b/w All I Want Is You
CD1 calendar sleeve return Remix b/w It Only Takes A Minute
(Live)/Give Good Feeling (Live)
CD2 Return Remix b/w All I Want Is You/Could It Be Magic
(Live)/Pray (Live)

Video director: Greg Masuak
Sleeve design: T&CP Associates
Sleeve photography: Mike Prior

EVERYTHING CHANGES
Words and music: Gary Barlow, Mike Ward, Eliot Kennedy and
Cary Baylis
Producers: Mike Ward and Eliot Kennedy for Five Boys Productions
Additional production and guitar: Cary Baylis
Mixed by: Eliot Kennedy
Engineers: Peter Stewart and Alan Fisch
UK release: March 1994 on RCA
7", MC b/w Beatles Medley
CD1 b/w Beatles Medley/Everything Changes (Nigel Lowis
Mix)/Everything Changes (Extended Version)
CD2 Nigel Lowis Remix b/w Interview/Relight My Fire (Live)

Video director: Greg Masuak
Sleeve design: T&CP Associates
Sleeve photographer: Katerina Jebb

LOVE AIN'T HERE ANYMORE
Words and music: Gary Barlow
Producers: S&P Jervier and J Wales
Additional vocal production: Mark Beswick
Engineer: Pete Craigie
UK release: June 1994 on RCA
CD1 b/w The Party Remix/Another Crack In My Heart
(Live)/Everything Changes (TOTP satellite performance)
CD2 Live b/w Rock'n'Roll Medley (Live)/Wasting My Time (Live)
Babe (Live)
MC1 b/w The Party Remix/Everything Changes (TOTP satellite
performance)
MC2 Live b/w Rock'n'Roll Medley (Live)/Babe (Live)

Video directors: Liam Kan and Grant Hodgson
Sleeve design: T&CP Associates
Sleeve photographer: Katerina Jebb

SURE
Words and music: Gary Barlow, Robbie Williams and Mark Owen
Producers: Brothers in Rhythm for DMC (UK) Ltd
Mixed by: Howard Bargroff, assisted by Alan Bremner and Andy
Gallimore
UK release: October 1994 on RCA
CD1 b/w Thumpers Club Mix/Full Pressure Club Mix/Strictly Barking
Dub
CD2 b/w No Si Aqui No Hay Amor/Why Can't I Wake Up With You

(Club Mix)/You Are The One (Tonik Mix)
MC b/w No Si Aqui No Hay Amor
12" Thumpers Club Mix b/w Brothers In Rhythm Mix/Full Pressure Mix

Video director: Greg Masuak
Sleeve design: T&CP Associates
Sleeve photography:Valerie Phillips

BACK FOR GOOD
Words and music: Gary Barlow
Producers: Chris Porter and Gary Barlow
Assistant engineer: Steve McNichol
UK release: March 1995 on RCA
CD1 Radio Mix b/w Sure (Live)/Beatles Tribute (Live)
CD2 Radio Mix b/w Pray/ Why Can't I Wake Up With You /A Million
Love Songs
MC Radio Mix b/w Sure (Live)/Back For Good (TV Mix)

Video directors: Vaughan and Anthea
Sleeve design: Morgan Penn
Sleeve photography: Andy Earl

NEVER FORGET
Words and music: Gary Barlow
Producers: Jim Steinman, Dave James and Brothers in Rhythm
Mixed by: Howard Bargroff, assisted by Alan Bremner and Andy
Gallimore
UK release: July 1995 on RCA
CD1 b/w Back For Good (Live)/Babe (Live)
CD2 b/w Interview

Video director: David Amphlett
Sleeve design: Morgan Penn
Sleeve photography: Philip Ollerenshaw

HOW DEEP IS YOUR LOVE
Words and music: Barry, Robin and Maurice Gibb
Producer: Chris Porter and Take That
Release date: February 1996 on RCA
CD1 b/w Every Guy (Live)/Lady Tonight (Live)/Sunday to Saturday(Live)
CD2 b/w Back for Good (Live)/Babe (Live)/Never Forget (Live)
MC b/w Never Forget (Live)

Video director: Nicholas Brandt
Sleeve design: Morgan Penn
Sleeve photography: Philip Ollerenshaw

ACKNOWLEDGMENTS

The Publishers would like to thank the following organisations for their kind permission to include the lyrics of the songs in this book:

Do What U Like Words and Music by Gary Barlow and Ray Hedges
© 1991 Reproduced by permission of EMI Virgin Music Ltd, London

Promises Words and Music by Gary Barlow and Graham Stack
© 1991 Reproduced by permission of EMI Virgin Music Ltd, London, Zomba Music Publishers Ltd

Once You've Tasted Love Words and Music by Gary Barlow
© 1992 Reproduced by permission of EMI Virgin Music Ltd, London

A Million Love Songs Words and Music by Gary Barlow
© 1992 Reproduced by permission of EMI Virgin Music Ltd, London

Why Can't I Wake Up With You Words and Music by Gary Barlow
© 1992 Reproduced by permission of EMI Virgin Music Ltd, London

Pray Words and Music by Gary Barlow

© 1993 Reproduced by permission of EMI Virgin Music Ltd, London

Babe Words and Music by Gary Barlow
© 1993 Reproduced by permission of EMI Virgin Music Ltd, London

Everything Changes Words and Music by Gary Barlow, Eliot Kennedy, Cary Baylis and Michael Ward
© 1993 Reproduced by permission of EMI Virgin Music Ltd, London, Chrysalis Music Ltd, and Sony Music Publishing Ltd

Love Ain't Here Anymore Words and Music by Gary Barlow
© 1993 Reproduced by permission of EMI Virgin Music Ltd, London

Sure Words and Music by Gary Barlow, Robert Williams and Mark Owen
© 1994 Reproduced by permission of EMI Virgin Music Ltd, London

Back for Good Words and Music by Gary Barlow
© 1994 Reproduced by permission of EMI Virgin Music Ltd, London

Never Forget Words and Music by Gary Barlow
©1993 Reproduced by permission of EMI Virgin Music Ltd, London

PICTURE CREDITS

The following photographs supplied by Idols Licensing & Publicity Ltd © Take That
Philip Ollerenshaw 2, 4, 5, 6, 8, 9, 10,11, 12, 13, 14, 15, 18, 20, 21, 22, 23, 24, 25, 28, 29, 33, 34, 35, 36, 40, 41, 43, 46, 47, 50, 51, 52, 53, 54, 55, 56, 57, 60, 61, 62, 63, 64, 65, 66, 67, 68-69, 70, 71, 72, 73, 74, 75, 76, 77, 78, 79, 80, 81, 82, 83, 84, 85, 86-87, 88, 89, 90, 91, 92 (bottom), 93, 98, 99, 100, 101, 104, 105, 106, 107, 108, 109, 112
Tom Howard 42, 92 (top)
Robert Walker 1, 94,
Sandi Hodkinson 95, 96, 97

Other photographs by
Chris Taylor - thanks to TV Hits 44, 45
James Martin 26, 27, 30, 31, 32
Take That and families 102,103
André Lansel 58, 59
Paul Cox 19
Dean Freeman 48, 49

All single sleeves except Do What U Like reproduced courtesy of RCA Records/BMG (UK) Ltd. Do What U Like courtesy of NMS Management Ltd

Every effort has been made to acknowledge correctly and contact the source and/or copyright holder of each photograph and Virgin Publishing Ltd apologises for any unintentional errors or omissions which will be corrected in future editions of the book.